I0621650

AN ASPEN CREEK CHRISTMAS, BOOK THREE

SHEILA'S Christmas BLESSING

LINORE ROSE BURKARD

LILLIPUT PRESS

SHEILA'S CHRISTMAS BLESSING: AN ASPEN CREEK CHRISTMAS, BOOK 3

EPUB ISBN: 978-1-955511-17-9

PPBK ISBN: 978-1-955511-26-1

Fiction: Christmas Romance, Christian Romance, Contemporary Romance, Sweet and Wholesome, Married-Couple Romance

Previous Volumes in This Series:

Emma's Christmas Surprise

Tessa's Christmas Joy

Contents

Reader, Please Note

THE FIRST THREE VOLUMES in An Aspen Creek Christmas Series cover the month of December. Unlike other series, they cover the *same* month but from three different perspectives.

Beginning in 2026, the next volume, *Rosa's Christmas Promise* will pick up where Sheila leaves off and continue in time like other series.

What does this mean for you? *Sheila's Christmas Blessing* can be read as a stand-alone novella, but you'll enjoy it more if you read the books that came first.

Thank you so much for your support. *You* are why writing is worthwhile.

All glory to God, who gives me words and ideas that turn into stories, and with much appreciation for you, my reader. I wish you blessings at Christmas and at any other time.

And now, enjoy the story!

Lenore Rose Burkard

THEMES

Trusting God, no matter how bleak the circumstances, leads to the best possible outcome.

Love and honesty go hand in hand.

Chapter One

THE PROBLEM

Aspen Creek, Pennsylvania, December

The front door opened with a jingle of Christmas bells, ruining Sheila Preston's hopes of sneaking into the house unobserved. She loved this time of year and had strung Christmas lights and faux greenery along the porch, but she forgot about the bells.

As she entered, the kids came charging up from the basement shouting, "Mom's home!" Her mother, Joanie Henderson, would be right behind them. She'd see that the groceries Sheila was carrying were from the church common room, an in-house food pantry, not the grocery store. Her lips would purse in disapproval.

Kacie was home for Christmas break and Mrs. Henderson didn't mind watching her and Jase twice a week while Sheila did errands and shopped. But her presence came with a cost.

She hurried to the kitchen with the slim hope of putting things away before her mother saw them. Jase and Kacie barreled in.

"Mommy! Mommy!" Four-year-old Jase hugged her left leg. Seven-year-old Kacie hopped up and down, waiting to be greeted.

"Hi guys!" she smiled and planted a kiss on each of their heads. "Did you have fun with Grandma?"

Neither answered, but Kacie peeked excitedly at the groceries. "What'd you get, Mom? What'd you get?"

"Go into the living room with Grandma and wait for me. You'll see later."

"I wanna see what you got!" Kacie's oval face scrunched into a frown.

"Later," Sheila said curtly.

Her mother appeared in the doorway, her eyes narrowing at the box of fresh vegetables in clear zip-lock plastic bags, and the frozen raw meat in gallon-size ones, shouting they were not store packages. She folded her arms and leaned against the wall.

Mrs. Henderson was a cultured, well-dressed woman, slim, neat, and dignified. She'd been wealthy all her life and though she hid it, she looked down on the less well-to-do. Sheila knew she thought poor people were lazy.

Her parents hadn't approved of her marrying Ryan Preston. He'd been framed as a drug dealer, and though innocent, did a brief stint in prison. Her mother never believed he was innocent. Now that he'd lost his job and been out of work for months, she felt they'd been right.

Ryan had brought Kacie, then only an infant, to the marriage, which they counted as another mark against him. They knew he had questioned Kacie's paternity and that his ex-girlfriend had succumbed to drug addiction and abandoned the baby.

Both the out-of-wedlock baby and the association with drugs were grave failings they couldn't seem to get past—at least in her mother's case. She considered him a loser, unworthy of her daughter.

And he knew it.

Her mother said with a frown, "C'mon, Kace and Jase—let's go find something to do while your mother puts things away."

"I wanna see what she got!" Kace repeated. Sheila's mother herded her out with a little push against her back. "You will, later."

Sheila sighed and returned to unboxing the food. It was a godsend to have a church with a food pantry. Ryan had been a good provider until this year. Ten months ago, he was passed over for a promotion he deserved that would have made him a top executive in Blue Star, the firm he worked for. Two weeks later, he was fired by the guy who got it.

Ryan's faith took a blow, and over time it was clear that their marriage and family had also. Paying for a health plan was eating up their savings. Add the mortgage and other bills, and how long could they get by? Ryan did the banking and assured Sheila they were still okay, but she'd started using a credit card just in case. She'd been raised to despise and avoid debt. She wondered if soon it would be the only way to survive.

She'd never been poor. She couldn't imagine living on welfare and food stamps, but if Ryan didn't do something soon... *Oh, Ryan!* She pushed away the worries. She could live scrimping to get by. Millions of people did. But hardest to bear was the change in her formerly steadfast, good-natured husband.

The unfairness of getting fired and the spitefulness of a former co-worker had landed hard on him. He couldn't understand why God had allowed it to happen, and his bewilderment grew as the months went by and no suitable position turned up.

He'd grown moody and often missed church. Then, about two months ago, he began disappearing early in the morning, often staying out late, and not revealing where he'd been or what he'd been up to.

She didn't like to grill him about it. He was sensitive to anything she said, any questions she asked, he felt she was accusing him of being a failure. The littlest doubt she expressed about their welfare sent him into a silent retreat, as if he believed she agreed with her parents' assessment of him.

She never had. She saw the best in Ryan, always. Even now she tried to believe that despite his secrecy and moodiness, he was still the faithful, loyal husband she'd married, one who wanted to take excellent care of his wife and family—even if he hadn't been able to do that of late. She *needed* to believe he was still that man.

An animated movie started in the living room. Kace appeared in the doorway. "Mommy, come watch with us!"

"I have to start dinner, honey," she said.

Mrs. Henderson appeared behind Kace. "I brought dinner. It's in the refrigerator, pot roast and potatoes, fully cooked. Just heat it in the oven for about an hour and add a vegetable."

"Thanks, Mom," she said, but her heart sank. That her mom had begun bringing meals was a telltale sign that she knew they were in financial straits. To Sheila, each dish came with an unspoken message: "*I made this because of your failure of a husband. We tried to tell you, but you didn't listen. You never should have married him.*"

As the months of unemployment dragged on, her efforts at hiding their worsening condition had been in vain. She supposed it was inevitable her parents would know because every time they inquired if Ryan found a job, her answer was always the same. Not yet.

Her mother opened the refrigerator, took out the food, and placed it on the counter. "Best let it sit for fifteen minutes before reheating." She paused. "I also put a few things in the freezer for later."

"Thanks, but you didn't have to do that."

"Oh, I think I did," she said. She nodded curtly, her lips still compressed. "Guess I'll be off. Your dad needs to eat too."

"Send my love to Dad. And thanks for watching the kids."

"That's what grandmothers are for," Mrs. Henderson said, though her tone wasn't jovial. She stepped toward the counter, looking over the last few packages not yet stashed out of sight. Sheila waited for the reproof. "Well?"

"Well what? Do you think I'm surprised you need a food pantry?"

"It's from the common room at church, and primarily just for the church. All of us at Grace use it," Sheila said. "They tell us to, or it will go bad."

"Mm-hmm."

"They do, Mom!"

"I believe you. I wasn't going to say anything," she said airily, her brows raised. She pursed her lips. "When does that husband of yours get home?"

"In time for dinner." Sheila hoped it was true. "We eat around 5:30. Sure you don't want to stay and eat with us?"

Her mother shook her head. "Your father would be alone."

While Jase and Kace gave goodbye hugs to Grandma, Sheila preheated the oven and moved her mom's pot roast into a roasting pan. She wished—for the thousandth time—that Ryan hadn't lost his job, that he'd never been unjustly convicted, that her parents could see how good a man he was, even now.

He'd given his life to Christ a year before their marriage. He had a good job at a small construction firm back then and was a faithful attender at the men's weekly Bible study. He was often around to help at church events.

Was. Again, she brushed away doubts as to whether he was still that man.

Mrs. Henderson got her coat from the closet and stood, looking smart and stylish, pulling on leather gloves. She met Sheila's eyes appraisingly. "How much can we loan you?" she asked.

"What?" Sheila blinked, confused. She hadn't asked for a loan.

"Well, you need help, don't you? We'll loan you up to ten thousand."

"Thank you but no," Sheila said firmly. "We don't need your money." She tried to suppress the resentment she felt. Her parents were only trying to help.

Her mother huffed. "I saw your pantry and refrigerator. You do need it. For goodness' sake, honey, it's Christmas time. These children shouldn't have to suffer for the sins of the father."

Kace and Jase's heads popped up and they stared, wide-eyed, at the women.

"Mom, please!" Sheila returned in an undertone. "I already found nice things for them."

Her mother looked away and then back with an annoyed expression. "Look, it's just a loan until Ryan gets his act together. We'd give it to you outright if we thought you'd accept it but I figured you wouldn't."

Sheila didn't deny it. "Get home safe." Maybe if she wouldn't talk about it her mother would give up and leave.

"How long can you go on without a working man in the house?" Mrs. Henderson stepped closer and softened her voice. "Of course you need help. We can give you whatever you need until he—until he mans up and starts providing for you again."

"Mom! Don't pick on Ryan, okay? We have savings." Her heart was racing. "He's got a plan."

"What's his plan?" she asked plaintively. "What does he do all day if he's not here and he's not working?" Mrs. Henderson had asked this same question before, always with furrowed brows and the lines in her face deepening.

"He is working at *something.*" Sheila knew as she spoke that it sounded like a lame excuse. It was all Ryan would tell her, and it probably was an excuse. Why he was gone all day, six days a week, she did not know.

Maddeningly, her mother persisted. "What's he working at?" She stared at Sheila accusingly because they both knew she had no idea what her husband was up to.

How could she know when he wouldn't say? She resisted a sense of despair.

"He says it's a surprise. And I'm thinking of getting a job myself," she said, crossing her arms.

"And not stay home with these children?" Her mother's tone was scandalized.

"Kace will be back in school in January, and there are good preschools in the area," Sheila began.

"I thought you were going to look into homeschooling instead of giving these precious souls to strangers." Her hands were on her hips now.

"Kace loves school. And I can work when they're in class. They have to be watched by someone!" Sheila's voice was dangerously close to cracking.

"Yes, and it ought to be *you.* I can watch them twice a week, but no more than that." She pursed her lips, frowning. "Find out what that man of yours is up to, will you?" She shook her head. "If we at least thought he was searching, doing *something,* heck, he could work at Wal-Mart until something better turns up. But to be doing *nothing*!"

Sheila glanced uneasily at Kace, who was all ears. "Kace, honey, run and get me Jase's favorite blankie."

Kace frowned but started off as instructed.

Sheila turned to her mother. "Mom, he's doing something, I told you. He wants to surprise me, that's all. He won't tell me until whatever it is, is ready, whatever that means."

Her mother turned to go but stopped at the door and looked back. "Is he giving you any money in the meantime? That's what matters. And how do you know he's not going back—" she stopped and adjusted her purse.

Sheila stared at her tragically. She knew the unfinished words, "to dealing drugs."

"He *never* did that. How many times do I have to tell you it was a false conviction? He was framed!"

"Men who spend time in prison learn all kinds of underhanded ways to make money," she said, wrapping her scarf around her neck.

"Not Ryan," Sheila said tersely, believing with all her heart that she was right.

Chapter Two

BEST FRIENDS ARE FOR SHARING

ON SATURDAY MORNING, SHEILA'S best friend Emma Dawson arrived to pick her up for their monthly day of lunch and shopping.

While Sheila went over instructions with Clara, the babysitter, Emma cleared the breakfast dishes from the table and washed what couldn't go in the dishwasher.

Clara was a lovely young woman with thick brown hair past her shoulders, friendly eyes behind glasses, and a pretty, if shy, smile. She was also an angel. A college student from church, she assured Sheila she'd be happy to watch the kids at no charge. She was studying for a future career in child psychology, so it gave her an opportunity to gain experience with kids.

They couldn't afford a sitter, and her mother was involved in a ladies' club on Saturdays, so Clara's offer was received gratefully. It used to be that Ryan would happily watch the kids on such days and send her off with a kiss. Nowadays, he was already gone and wouldn't return until evening.

She missed the old days when bargain-hunting with Emma was for fun, not necessity. Today, they'd shop at Aspen Valley Thrift and maybe the Hearth & Quill Used Books. Lightly used books that looked brand new could make great gifts, and they also sold puzzles, toys and other small novelties.

In the past, they might watch an occasional matinee afterward—if they could find something clean in the theater, and the kids didn't get too upset by her absence.

Sheila didn't do movies anymore, both to save money and because she didn't want to take advantage of Clara by staying out too long. Emma was having dinner later with Gabe, her boyfriend, anyway. Gabe Huskman, their pastor-intern, was a good man, though not very fun, in Sheila's opinion.

Emma turned onto Main Street, slowing to the mandatory twenty-five miles per hour. They wouldn't have wanted to rush anyway, as meandering gave them a chance to relish the sights. Main Street was a storybook sight in winter, especially before Christmas.

All of Aspen Creek was like a fairy tale this time of year because the town went all out with its Christmas décor. Nowhere more than here on Main Street. It was comforting and cozy, like stepping into a Dickens novel. Combined with a recent snowfall, it was picture perfect.

"Don't you love it?" Sheila said, referring to the magical feeling of holiday warmth she never got tired of. As it washed over her as if for the first time, she thanked God for where she lived.

Emma knew what she meant. "I do! I'm glad you could do this with me today."

A large banner hanging across the road welcomed them to Aspen Creek, "The Village of Holiday Hospitality." Further down the street, a second banner wished them "A Warm and Wonderful Merry Christmas." At the far end of the street, a third banner proclaimed, "Jesus is the Reason for the Season."

The previous year, the Becketts, a couple who owned the Porchlight Hotel, had proposed a motion at a town meeting to have that last banner removed, calling it propaganda for religion.

The town board turned them down, reasoning that since Christmas was based on the birth of Christ—there would be no Christmas without that event—it wasn't propaganda but a fact, and that was that.

The Becketts, nevertheless, went house to house gathering signatures to support their motion. Another couple, the owners of Blue Willow Antiques, started a counter petition. Sheila and Ryan resided outside the town proper and so their signatures wouldn't count, but they gave their whole-hearted support to keeping the banner, telling everyone they knew about the petition.

In the end, the Becketts were able to garner only a handful of signatures and there died the motion.

Sheila, Ryan, the majority of residents, and all of Grace Church were glad. They were happier to learn, subsequently, that the Board voted not to consider such a motion again for at least six years. The Reason for the Season was welcome in Aspen Creek.

Sheila continued to soak in the seasonal atmosphere like taking a breath of fresh mountain air. Green garlands intertwined with white lights circled the old-fashioned lampposts standing like quaint sentinels all the way down the street. Foot-high light-up snowflakes perched at their tops.

They stopped at a light and were able to admire the single white gazebo that stood on the north side of the street. It sheltered a big Christmas tree strewn with lights and oversized ornaments. After dark, it blazed so brightly you could see the glow a block or two away.

Her family had missed the tree-lighting ceremony this year, but she'd be sure to bring the kids through the town one night to let them see it all lit up in the dark.

Would Ryan be with them? Not if he kept staying out late. Her heart ached at the thought. If she knew what he was doing, that might help. Why was he so stubbornly secretive about it?

AT ASPEN VALLEY THRIFT, it alarmed Sheila how quickly her purchases added up. Brand new socks for the kids for their Christmas stockings, a sweet hat and mitten set with attached pom-poms that Kace would adore, and a winter coat for Jase, who was still using last year's though he'd grown two inches.

She hesitated over a dress shirt for Ryan. It was new and still had the store tag and was the kind he'd always worn when working. In warmer months, he switched to short-sleeved shirts with a pocket—even weekend t-shirts had to have a pocket for a pen. He filled both styles handsomely with his broad shoulders and neck.

Lately he favored plaid flannel shirts. He wore them when he left the house, which meant that whatever he was doing, it wasn't another office job.

She bought the shirt anyway, hoping it would show she still had faith in him to provide for them. He might take it as a hint that she wanted him to get another office job—and in a way, she did. There was stability in that.

At Hearth and Quill, Sheila picked up some used paperback classics for the kids, as well as inexpensive puzzles, stickers and fun bookmarks. They weren't broke yet, and if ever there was a time when she liked to shower the kids with gifts, it was Christmas.

God had showered his love on the earth by sending His Son. Aside from East-er—Resurrection Day, as Grace Church called it—it was the most important holiday of the year, and she wanted the kids to know it.

Emma suggested popping into Amy's Amish Quilts, where its windows beckoned with red and green quilts, cheery pillows, framed Scripture verses, knickknacks and boxed cookies. It was the perfect place to browse and relax while chatting with the two big-hearted Amish ladies, Amy and "Sunshine," as they called Amy's daughter.

But her purchases had drained her inner 'spending allowance' for the day. The store wasn't fun when you were feeling broke.

She said, "I spent too much already. I need to get there soon for our chocolates, but I'll do it another day." Every year, she bought one box of the ladies' hand-crafted, specialty mixed chocolates for the family. She brought it out either on Christmas Eve or after Christmas dinner, and it was now a family tradition. At $29.99 a box, it was a splurge, and in the past, they could afford it. This year, she'd have to think twice about it.

"I love those chocolates! Do you want to charge it in case they run out? Last year, they did."

Sheila sighed. "I guess I could, but I don't want to right now." She was going to charge her lunch as it was. She paused, considering. Bundled up pedestrians passed by and Emma rubbed her gloved hands together. It was too cold to stand there thinking about it.

"Another time," she said, moving them along toward their favorite café, Maple & Main. "It'll give me a reason to come down and browse again."

They pulled their scarves tighter against the cold. Sheila shivered but enjoyed the feel of it—Christmas was in the air.

She and Emma deposited their finds into the trunk of her car, and proceeded to Maple & Main with its cozy booths and cheery atmosphere.

The café was decorated with garland, bows, and strings of twinkling lights. Carols played softly in the background, and it lifted Sheila's heart and gave the perfect warm Yuletide atmosphere.

Before Alicia, their cheerful, plus-sized waitress came to take their order, however, they detected other background sounds: muffled noises, hammering, things moving. Sounds of construction, perhaps.

"Didn't we hear a little of that the last time we were here?" Sheila asked. "I wonder what's going on."

When Alicia appeared, menus in hand, she gushed, "Well, how are two of my favorite ladies?"

Smiling, Sheila said, "How is our favorite waitress?" This was a running joke, since they always greeted each other this way, and since Alicia was the only waitress in the café. Maple & Main only stayed open until 2:30 pm, and if it got too busy, Amber, the cafe's owner, helped with the serving.

Emma asked, "Is there building going on?" She motioned toward the sounds.

"Oh," Alicia gushed, waving her hand down dismissively, "sorry about that. You haven't heard? The owners are expanding! When it's done, this wall will be gone and open to the new area with a book and gift shop, a full coffee and latte bar, you know, the whole works!"

She grinned and leaned in conspiratorially. "It'll be fun, but I expect Maple & Main will be a lot busier. And our hours are expanding too."

"Will it be done in time for Christmas?" Sheila asked out of polite curiosity.

"Amber hopes so." Amber Branson and her husband were the owners, but only Amber spent time at the café. "The builder says he can do it." Alicia shrugged. "Guess we'll find out!" She leaned in to whisper, "Between us, I hope it's not. The last thing I want right now is to work longer days, even though the extra money would be nice."

Emma and Sheila nodded understandingly. Alicia had taken in a ten-year-old niece when her sister died unexpectedly. She was in the process of adopting her.

With one plump hand on the table, she added, "They'll have to hire more help, and that's all there is to it."

Her usual cheery smile returned. She pulled out a small notepad and pencil. "Now, what can I get you ladies?"

They ordered bowls of steaming soup and an accompanying side. Emma added an eggnog hot chocolate, and Sheila a smothered brownie.

"Great choices!" Alicia gushed. "I love that hot chocolate."

"It has way too much sugar," Emma said, grinning. "But I love it too."

Sheila grinned back "I'm sure my brownie has more sugar than your cocoa." She also added a cup of holiday chai tea to her order.

Alicia surveyed them. "I almost forgot. How was the bargain hunting today? I am so behind on Christmas shopping," she added, shaking her head. While Sheila and Emma filled her in on what Valley Thrift and the bookstore had in stock and the gifts they'd bought, she listened intently, nodding at intervals.

"That sounds good. Did you get to that new consignment shop? It's a big room off the entrance of Porchlight Hotel. I think it's called The Welcome Closet."

"I didn't know about it," Emma said.

Sheila hadn't either. She said, "Maybe we can check it out soon."

"If I get there, I'll let you know what I think," Alicia said.

Shortly after she left, the Christmas carols in the background went up a notch and the construction noise from next door went down. The ladies shared a grin. But Sheila's mind was abuzz with the thought that there was a construction outfit in town. Just the kind of place Ryan should apply to work for!

She must have looked pensive. Emma's face grew serious and her eyes searched Sheila's. "You seem gloomy. Is everything all right?"

Sheila knew the unspoken words at the end of that question: *with Ryan*. She took a sip of her drink and to her surprise, her heart started bubbling like a geyser about to burst. She needed to talk. She put the cup down and looked at Emma. "He's been gone again every day this week, almost all day, and still won't say where he's been or what he's doing."

"Not again!" Emma cried. Her face scrunched with genuine distress. "I thought you were going to talk to him."

Sheila shook her head. "I try to. He won't talk to me. Everything I say he takes the wrong way, as if just asking a question means I have no faith in him at all."

She took a bite of brownie and swallowed. She realized that her faith, the fuel that kept her heart hoping despite Ryan's stubborn secrecy, was crumbling. As if it had gone a long time ago, gone with the Ryan she loved, she said something she didn't even realize she'd been thinking.

"Honestly, Em, I'm this close," she held up two fingers almost touching, "to asking for a divorce." Shocked at her own words, she added, "I want to scare him! I'm beginning to wonder if he's doing something illegal or—or gambling or something."

Emma's eyes filled with pain and concern. She took a deep breath, as if she couldn't believe what Sheila had said any more than Sheila could. Frowning, she said, "Because of his secrecy? Don't think the worst. Your husband's going through a hard time, but he's a good man. Gabe says so, too." She paused and then added, "Don't ask for something you don't really want."

Sheila knew she would never ask for a divorce, not unless Ryan was unfaithful. She didn't even know where those words had come from. And she did not truly believe that he would resort to something illicit, certainly not gambling. She scolded herself for speaking so negatively about him.

"I didn't mean that about Ryan," she said, shaking her head. "I'm sure he'll come around and tell me everything like he says he will. It's just so hard not to know what's going on. And to wait for things to improve."

She patted the back of her head, thinking. "No matter how late he comes in, he jumps right into the shower. I don't know if that's because he's doing manual labor, or because he can leave without showering in the morning."

He hadn't done that when he had his office job.

Emma listened, nodding while "Hark! The Herald Angels Sing" wafted out around them.

"I've tried insisting he open up to me, but he always manages to weasel his way out of telling me anything." Sheila huffed out a breath. "And he makes me feel guilty for asking!"

Emma leaned forward across the little table they occupied, "Weren't you two gonna talk to Mark?"

Their pastor, Mark Grant, was a professional counselor. "We did. We had one counseling session and Ryan hasn't agreed to another. I don't think he's going to. Mark told him the Bible says, 'If a man doesn't work, neither should he eat.' And 'If a man doesn't provide for his own family, he's worse than an infidel.' That made him *so* mad."

She mimicked his voice. "It wasn't MY idea to get fired! I should have had a good raise. I helped that company! I WANT to provide for my family. God is the one blocking me from doing it!"

Emma's face sobered. She touched Sheila's hand and gave it a squeeze. "I'll keep praying for you. And him."

"I know you will." Sheila sipped her tea. She hadn't realized how deeply alarmed she was over the state of things. But she didn't want to spend her time with Emma focusing on that. She took another sip, swallowed her angst with the brew, and cried, "Enough about him! This is our day, and I won't let him spoil it. How's it going with Gabe? Has he dropped any more hints about proposing?"

Emma's lips curved up. "He said he has a Christmas surprise for me."

Sheila raised a brow. "Oh my! You think that's when he's going to pop the question?"

Emma said, "That's what I'm thinking."

Sheila lowered her head and looked at Emma through her lashes. Gabe did not strike her as the perfect match for her friend. "Has he at least kissed you again?" she asked. Emma had told her that they'd only shared one good kiss, and they'd been dating for eleven months!

She repressed an embarrassed smile. "No."

Sheila's lips pursed. "Look, I know you've said you're not looking for romance, and I applaud you for that. My Ryan is the perfect example of why you shouldn't. All those dinners, flowers and candy." She sighed, remembering how sweet and swoony he was back then. She had enjoyed it all, the restaurant dates, surprise bouquets at her doorstep, boxes of chocolates.

These days, at times, he was still sweet and swoony, but it felt disingenuous when he wasn't being open with her. "He was Mr. Romantic himself and look how he turned out now."

She shouldn't have said that. In her heart, Sheila believed her sweet, good husband was still there. He was going through a trial, that's all. Some trials took a good while to play out.

Emma nodded. "Remember Jared from the worship team? He bought me jewelry and took me to ballets and concerts, and then wanted me to sleep with him! I refused and he disappeared." She shook her head. "Romance is a scam."

Sheila looked thoughtful. She liked a little romance now and then. Marriage didn't change that. "Well, it certainly isn't everything," she said. "But are you sure Gabe's the right guy for you? Mr. *Un*romantic?" She continued, "And how many guys don't even give the woman they plan on proposing to a real, good kiss?"

Smiling dreamily she added, "All Ryan would have to do is give me one, you know, a nice, slow kiss, and I'd want to forgive him everything." Her face sobered. "Until it's over. Then I'd remember he's still not being square with me. And frankly, we haven't had kisses like that lately."

Emma stirred her cocoa. "I'm sorry. And as for Gabe, well, I don't know for sure that he's going to propose."

Sheila didn't want to insult her friend, but she felt in case a proposal was on its way, Emma needed to think very carefully before accepting it. Before making a huge mistake. *Was she beginning to wonder if she had made one? That her parents were right after all?*

Emma listed off Gabe's good qualities, highlighting his strong faith and walk with God. Sheila nodded. "Those *are* good things." She stopped to take another bite of smothered brownie. She swallowed and said, "I wish I'd looked deeper for that in Ryan. Attending church on Sunday does not a true Christian make. He was faithful in Bible Study, and I thought he loved the Lord...but now I don't know."

Frowning, she continued, "He doesn't even attend regularly anymore. I know you've noticed."

Emma again placed a hand upon one of hers to give it a sympathetic squeeze.

"All I want," Sheila said leaning forward, is the Ryan I married. The man who had unwavering faith in Jesus, the attentive father and husband who lived for his family, who could hold down a good job and bring home a paycheck. The man my parents could *see* is a good man."

"Did they ever see it?" Emma asked abruptly, as if she knew they had not.

Sheila hesitated. She had to admit that no matter how great a husband, father and provider Ryan was, her parents had never really acknowledged it. Her dad liked Ryan and was more accepting, but their behavior now, especially that of her mother, showed they felt justified, as if behind every visit were the words, "He's no good, and we told you so."

When Alicia brought two checks, Emma whipped both from her hand. "I've got it," she said.

"You don't have to, Em," Sheila protested. "I'm ready to charge it."

"No way," she said, with a grin. "You already spent enough today."

Emma was such a sweet friend. Sheila hated to see her so cut up about whether or not to marry Gabe. She enjoyed Gabe, even admired him, but he didn't exactly set her heart racing.

Sheila thanked her for the lunch, and, before they left, told her, "Marriage lasts a long time. Be sure, be very sure, Em, before saying 'yes.'"

Chapter Three

CAN WE TALK?

SHEILA AWAKENED EARLY, DETERMINED to catch Ryan before he disappeared for the day as usual. She'd decided it was time to unearth whatever he was being so secretive about. She didn't like the insinuations her mother had made and couldn't deny they'd planted fear in her heart. Then, talking to Emma about it had made her decide this situation needed to end. Yesterday.

When she'd questioned him before, he told her to trust him. He was "working on something."

And she'd tried. But a man had to earn trust, and lately he wasn't behaving like a trustworthy person. Trustworthy people didn't keep their activities secret from their spouse.

She couldn't be expected to have the same trust in a man who wasn't the same.

Ryan had lost a job.

She felt as though she'd lost *him*.

She missed the security of their lives and future, so much of which depended on him working. They'd agreed it was best for the family if she stayed home so she'd always be available for the children. But when she told him she could get a job—she could go back to being a secretary—he got upset and said there was no need for that.

She wondered if that was going to change.

His quiet, steady breathing continued, so she took the opportunity to pray quietly.

Help me speak to him without getting upset, Lord. Help me reach his heart without making him defensive and more secretive. Help me show him that my faith hasn't faltered like his, but that openness in marriage is a must!

Ryan rolled to his side to face her, blinking. His muscular shoulders were above the sheets, and his chin bore the flirty shadow of a beard. Masculine. *Sexy.* She wished—no, it was no use. She stifled a pang of hurt. Their times together as man and wife had dwindled lately along with his presence in the home. That hurt, but his secrecy hurt more.

"Hey," he said.

"Good morning," she said, not trying to sound particularly pleasant. "The kids are still asleep. Will you have breakfast with me?"

He turned and faced the ceiling, yawned, and then turned back to her, reaching for her with one hand. "We could do other things with this time," he said, his lips twisting in the grin she usually found completely disarming. He rubbed her arm and then yanked playfully on it, pulling her toward him.

Sheila stiffened. She should want this—she longed for time with him, but how could she behave as though things were okay between them when he was living a secret life? Things were not okay. She'd tried to believe they were, but her mother's one suggestion had crumbled that illusion like a sandcastle melting in the tide.

"Is that all you have time for? I want to talk."

His lips pressed to a line and he turned back to face the ceiling. "Fine. Talk," he said, in a flat tone.

"I'll make coffee," she said, beginning to rise. "And then we'll talk."

He nodded, eyeing her heavily.

DOWNSTAIRS IN THE KITCHEN, Ryan joined her at the table where a steaming mug of coffee waited. Sheila noticed that he'd dressed in office attire. Had he found a job?

"Are we eating?" he asked. "Otherwise, I'd better get going so I have time to pick something up."

"What's your hurry?" she asked, more sharply than she'd intended. "Did you get a job?"

He sighed. "I've told you. I no longer want a job. I don't want to be somebody's *hire*. Somebody who can be fired at a whim."

"So what's your hurry?" she asked sardonically.

He put his cup down, slowly and carefully as if weighing his words. "You said you would trust me. I've always taken care of you and the kids. I've told you that you can buy as many groceries as before, you don't have to scrimp like you are."

"Our savings can't last forever," she countered. "I'm trying to stretch them." To eke out more information, she asked, "Do you have any idea how long I need to?"

He gazed at her, his lips pressed in a line. "This is going to work out. Just trust me."

A familiar angsty pain cut through her. "*Wha*t is going to work out? The part about you not wanting a job? Is that just going to work out? What does that look like?"

Frowning, he said tersely, "You'll see."

"Still? That's it? That's all you'll tell me? *You'll see*?"

His expression hardened. "I will tell you everything in time! Why don't you just admit that you don't trust me because I did time? You don't trust me because of my past."

"It's not that past that worries me," Sheila returned evenly. "It's the past months of you disappearing every day and not telling me what you're doing or where you're going. That's not what marriage is supposed to be!"

He shifted in his seat. "I know it's hard, Sheel. I get that." He paused. "But I'm not some stranger asking you to wait and trust. It's *me*. I *love* you. You should be glad I'm out every day, it means I'm doing something. I am going to prove that you can trust me, but you have to let me do it my way in my time."

Sheila grimaced. This wasn't going well. And she hated arguing. Miserably, she said, "You don't need to prove anything. Just that you haven't changed. That *we* haven't changed." She paused, surveying him. "Are you seeing another woman?"

Ryan shut his eyes and looked away, his lips compressed into a thin line. He turned back to her. "How can you ask me that? How can you even ask that?"

He was getting angry, Sheila could see that. But she was angry too. He stared at her as if she was the source of their troubles.

Her eyes filled with tears. "How can I not ask that? You leave this house every day but you won't share your life with me. You've—you've banned me from your life!"

"I haven't!" He sighed heavily, then came to his feet. He went around the table and started pulling her up from her chair. Sheila refused to cooperate and made him lift her. She'd never been skinny and described herself as "comfortable," but Ryan was a strong man.

With her feet on the ground, he put his arms around her and stared down into her eyes. "I love you. I will always love you." His head lowered and his mouth hovered near hers. She made no move to meet his lips with hers. He gave her a quick kiss.

"Can you just believe I'm going to come through for you and give me some room? Have we missed a mortgage payment? No. Are we paying the bills? Yes. I know we're going through money; I just need more time." He paused and looked at her with eyes clouded with hurt. 'But if you can't trust me, I don't know why you married me to begin with."

Sheila gazed up at him hopelessly. That felt unfair. "I married a different man," she said, blinking back sudden tears. "A man who shared his heart with me. A man I could know. And trust."

He stared at her for long seconds. "I'm still that guy. I'm going to take care of you. And the kids, and the house, all of it. As I've been saying, I have something in the works. Just *trust* me!"

She stared at him, her heart thumping. "Why should I trust you when you won't tell me anything?

He bit his lip, his eyes troubled. "I need to know you believe in me—even when you can't see why you should."

"Only God deserves that kind of trust!" she shot back.

He loosened his hold around her and picked up his cup and took it to the sink where he dumped the rest of its contents.

She spoke almost in a whisper. "Why can't you tell me what it is?"

He bit his lip as if biting back the first words that came to mind. Slowly he said, "Because trust means believing without seeing. If you trusted me, you wouldn't need to know."

Sheila closed her eyes to gather her thoughts and gain control of the emotions crashing like waves against rocks inside her. "Trustworthy people don't hide things."

His eyes hardened. "That's what you want to think. Fine. I knew it. I knew you never really had faith in me."

"That is not true!"

"It's true now. And that's what matters."

He moved away but then looked back. "It's like you think I'm just goofing off. Like you're just waiting for the police to show up for me or something."

"I am not! Your past has nothing to do with this!"

He looked struck, and then stared at the floor, thinking. When he looked back up, shaking his head, he said "You're wrong. It has everything to do with it."

They fell silent for long, long seconds. Sheila's anguish grew. She remembered the construction noise she'd heard with Emma at Maple & Main.

"There's construction going on in town. Maple & Main is expanding. Why can't you see if that company needs help? It's right up your alley."

His face blanched. He looked away and stretched his jaw. "I told you. I'm working on something."

Sheila was not hot-tempered, but this response sent her blood boiling. "Maybe I should take the kids and live with my parents. At least they will be honest with me! There, I'll know where I stand!"

He shook his head and walked off. She heard him open the front closet for his coat and gloves. Seconds later the front door opened with a jingle of Christmas bells and then shut. The cheery bells seemed like a mockery. This was supposed to be a wonderful time of year. Only it wasn't.

A strong cloud of hurt, disappointment and anger roiled in Sheila's stomach. He was so infuriating! She felt empty and alone.

Aloud she said, "I just want you back. The man I married. I want *us* back."

LATER THAT AFTERNOON WHEN she thought of the conversation, she realized how fed up with Ryan she was. Before this disastrous year, their married life had been wonderful. Even now, she thought wistfully, it still could be if he would just put everything out in the open, what he was up to, what he hoped to do, what his plan was. *Did he even have a plan?* She wanted to trust him, but his secrecy was making it impossible.

And then something unexpected occurred.

What about Me, the Holy Spirit seemed to whisper in her heart. *Can you trust Me despite all this? Can you trust Me not only to take care of you, Kacie and Jase, but Ryan as well?*

The question lingered in her heart for the rest of the day. That evening, praying aloud in her bedroom because the kids were asleep and Ryan wasn't home yet, she prayed, "I want to trust You, Lord, but how can I trust him when he's hiding so much? If You can just impress on Ryan that he's wrong to be secretive with me, it would make it a whole lot easier. Please help our marriage. Help Ryan to come around and be honest with me! Please show me what he's up to if he won't!"

She pressed her eyes to keep in tears that hovered beneath her lids. With a quavering voice, she added, "I will choose to trust You, Lord, with Ryan, with our needs as a family, and with our future—if You will help me do it. I feel like all I have is mustard seed faith. If You'll work with me with that, then I offer it to You. Thank You for being with me, and with us, through this."

Chapter Four

"I Only Need More Time"

RYAN COULD UNDERSTAND WHY Sheila was getting impatient. He'd lost his job ten months ago, their income had dropped abruptly, and she didn't know what he was doing to provide for them.

It didn't change the fact that he wasn't ready to tell her.

He needed her to trust him. If she loved him, couldn't she do that? If she trusted him, she wouldn't be unhappy or worried. He'd told her they would be okay, and while he was still uncertain his new venture would succeed, he wanted to sound confident for her sake.

After he'd been fired, he had wondered about his ability to succeed. If Sheila didn't believe in him, it meant she wondered too. Worse, she considered him a failure.

His parents hadn't believed in him. He'd been with the wrong crowd and got duped into holding what he thought was an innocent package for someone, only it was a kilo of cocaine. Someone tipped off the cops and he spent a year in jail for doing a guy a favor.

Lesson learned. Too late.

His parents never believed him innocent, and when he got home, they kicked him out. He hooked up with a girlfriend, Candy, whose drug use became an addiction. He was tempted to do the same—his parents had called him a drug addict, so why not live up to it? But he kept his wits about him and rejected that lifestyle. Still, he was lost and heading nowhere.

Giving his life to Jesus changed everything. Candy wanted no part of it and took off, leaving behind the infant she insisted was his, though Ryan doubted it. The timing didn't add up.

A Christian couple took him in along with baby Kacie, while he found a job in carpentry and construction. He discovered he liked working with his hands and building things. But he wanted to earn more. Night school, and eventually a degree in mechanical engineering and business management made that possible.

He moved up to a management position for Blue Star, a national home construction firm. His job wasn't to design or build homes, but to review designs they'd already commissioned, especially when buyers requested customizations. One of his jobs was to find ways to meet their requests with quality materials while containing costs.

He also reviewed whole house plans for cost efficiency, utilization of space, compliance to code, and so on, and all this in addition to managing a sales team.

When he met Sheila at church, he fell in love with her quickly. She was attractive, quick to smile, and honest almost to a fault—which he found refreshing. She didn't make him guess what she thought or how she felt. He liked that. She didn't play games.

Most of all, her easygoing nature charmed him. She accepted his past without a raised brow or darkened expression, and she accepted Kacie, too, despite his doubts about her paternity.

Before he proposed, it felt good to know he could take care of her and Kacie. When she said yes, the whole world felt good and right. Except for the Hendersons.

The only downside to his marriage were the Hendersons, Sheila's parents. Well, Doris, anyway. Discovering the past conviction meant he could do no right in her eyes. Like his parents, she believed the worst. Bill Henderson, her father, was much kinder, and had told Ryan confidentially that he believed in his innocence. He said his wife would come around, but Ryan had never seen evidence of that.

And now she felt justified in thinking him a loser.

He was beginning to think maybe she was right.

Before his firing, everything had been going great. Good job, marrying Sheel, the birth of Jase, buying their home, growing in their faith.

And then God let him down.

Why had He let it happen? His family could have been secure and happy for decades. He made a lucrative salary plus bonuses and was poised to move even higher at Blue Star. He'd been doing the right thing, calling out builders who were trying to cut corners with cheaper building materials and holding them accountable to the company's high standards. And what did he get for it? Fired! It was a gut-punch he hadn't seen coming.

They hadn't even let him go with unemployment benefits, claiming "wrongdoing" as the reason for his termination. Wrongdoing! When he'd been zealous for the company's good name and high standards!

It made him re-think his faith. Wasn't life supposed to get better with Jesus?

Financially, they were still okay, but their savings were being depleted. His wife viewed him as a loser, like his mother-in-law. His parents hardly spoke to him and considered him a lost cause to this day.

He'd cried to the Lord and hunted for a new job for months, but nothing turned up. It seemed a miracle now that Blue Star had hired him, for no other company was eager to. Slowly, he'd spiraled into depression. God wasn't listening to him anymore.

But one day he spotted a run-down building for sale in town. It was attached to Sheila's favorite café, Maple & Main. Strangely, it seemed to beckon to him.

Parking the car, he went to take a look from the outside. Only out of curiosity.

The owner saw him and came out, then offered to take him through the building. Ryan wasn't sure why, but he took him up on the offer.

As they walked through long-neglected rooms, Ryan's former job reading blueprints, spotting details, calculating costs without even realizing it, all kicked into gear. Before he knew it, he was mapping out a remodeled interior for the place in his mind.

He saw how the first floor could be turned into a café and grill where people could gather and socialize. Or he could make it into an efficient workspace for a small company. He could make it into a bookshop...a hair salon...a comfortable home.

The possibilities seemed endless. He was astonished at the ideas flowing across his brain as if they'd been there for ages waiting for a reason to come out.

His veins pumped with excitement. As the owner talked, he tried not to miss anything, particularly about the building and its history. As he went upstairs and saw more of it, the idea of a remodeling/renovation business grew. He'd use quality materials and transform rundown things into living spaces, useful and beautiful. Like bringing new life to dark places.

If the company took off, it would bring new life into *his* darkness.

Why hadn't he realized this sooner? When he'd totally remodeled and installed their kitchen at home, he'd been in his element, enjoying every step of the process. The planning as much as the actual work.

Ideas kept flowing. As if a light turned on inside him, he suddenly saw that eventually he could branch out into full home construction. He was familiar with how that worked.

More importantly, if he pulled this off, it would show Sheila he was worthy of her trust. It would vindicate him in the eyes of his parents and his mother-in-law.

There was one problem. Money. The owner didn't want a renovation, he wanted to sell. And if Ryan didn't grab the place soon, someone else would.

His heart pounded. He didn't want anyone else to get it.

He had no idea how, but he had to get that building.

Afterward, mulling it over, he realized he'd never run his own business. He'd helped manage one, sure, but starting a new one carried huge risks. And how could he start when he couldn't afford the building? He'd have to raise capital. He'd never done that before. With a police record, was it even possible?

The whole thing could be a colossal failure. If he took out loans and couldn't repay them, he and his family would end up in worse shape than they were already. He could just see the accusing faces of his parents, Doris, even Bill, and yes, Sheila too. They'd tell him he was a no-good loser just as they always thought.

He swallowed a lump in his throat. If he was the crying type, the very thought of Sheila accusing him if the business failed would bring him to tears. He could handle getting scorn from his folks and his in-laws.

But not from Sheel.

And that's when he knew he must not tell her his plan. He could not give her so much as a hint until he knew it would work. He couldn't stand it if she found out only to watch him fail at it the way he'd failed her this past year.

If she could just give him more time and some trust, it would make him feel like twice the man he was.

That shouldn't be too much to ask.

Chapter Five

CHURCH FRIENDS BRIELLE AND LEON

On Sunday morning, Ryan was in the kitchen when the kids came down to eat. They were excited because breakfast with Daddy on a Sunday morning was rare. Since he had dropped off going to church, he'd taken to sleeping in.

Kacie and Jase insisted that he make their eggs and toast, not even wanting Sheila to help. She hoped it would show Ryan how much they missed him.

They chattered about the fun Christmas projects they'd been working on and ran to get them to show their dad. Kacie had made a 2D colorful Nativity design using construction paper. With Sheila's help, Jase had made snowflake cut-outs with stencils and glued them to red and green construction paper.

At breakfast, Kacie said, "Daddy, are you coming with us to church today?"

Sheila winced inwardly. Kacie or Jase often asked her that. Most of the time, she had to say no. Nevertheless, they all looked at him expectantly.

Answering Kacie, he said, "Yup. I am, honey."

"Yay!" Kacie and Jase whooped and bounced in their seats. Jase waved his spoon in the air and tossed it toward the ceiling in his excitement. He missed it coming down and it clanged onto the floor.

"Pick it up," she said to him lightly. She felt glad about Ryan coming to church, but also cautious. He'd come now and then but it seemed to make no difference. Was he returning to his faith or was this one more visit to keep the kids happy?

Ryan swallowed a bite of scrambled egg and said, as if he knew her doubts, "I told Leon I'd see him there."

Sheila said, "Oh! You still talk with Leon?"

"I do."

She was glad to hear this. Leon Garcia, a tall, lanky light-brown man, was an engineer at a nearby air force base. Ryan's construction company had a contract with the base, and whenever they did work there—things Ryan wouldn't give details about because they were for the military and therefore guarded—he and Leon chatted. Ryan invited him to their church.

Leon resisted the invitation for a while but eventually showed up with his tall, beautiful girlfriend, Brielle Lightfoot. She and Sheila hit it off right from the start. Brielle was far more glamorous than Sheila, her makeup picture perfect, her complexion clear. She dressed with style and could have been a news anchor or even a model, but she was easygoing and friendly. That made her comfortable to be around. By contrast, Leon was serious and quiet, much like Ryan .

It was ironic—and sad—that Leon's attendance now was regular while Ryan's had dropped off.

"You're the reason he started coming to our church. He and Brielle are in membership classes."

"I know," he said, nodding. "And I guess now he's the reason I'm going back."

"God is the reason," she countered.

Ryan smirked. "Then he's using Leon."

She reached for his hand and squeezed it. "I'm glad. I'm glad you're coming."

He nodded. "I know."

When she went to zip up Jase's coat before leaving the house, Jase cried, "Let Daddy do it!"

"Yeah, let Daddy help us," echoed Kacie. She didn't need help at her age, but she waited with her coat unzipped, nevertheless.

Ryan obediently did the honors. He smiled for the children, but the look on his face afterward made Sheila think he *was* realizing how much his kids missed him. *Good.*

CHEERFUL CHATTER FROM THE back seat accompanied them for the ten-minute drive to Grace. As soon as they could, the kids barreled out of the car and headed toward the backlit life-size Nativity. It was centered in a snowy spot to the right of the Main doors, facing the street. The figures were wooden and fairly flat, but painted in bright, waterproof colors. With the lights and the stable, the posture of the kneeling shepherds and wise men holding out gifts, its reverential air felt just right for a church display.

Her kids always asked if they could try to pick up baby Jesus, and always they were told no, you couldn't pick him up, he was carved right into the manger.

Before service began, Emma sidled up to Sheila on her pew.

"Ryan's here!" she whispered. "I'm glad."

"That makes two of us," Sheila agreed, glancing over at her husband speaking with Ethan. "Ethan looks very suave today," she said, with a little smile.

Emma glanced at him but quickly looked away. "You don't have to tell me," she said miserably. "I've noticed, all too much."

Sheila leaned over. "It's not too much if you're meant for each other."

Emma's face looked wistful but she swallowed and her features hardened. "You're not helping me. I can't break Gabe's heart this close to Christmas, and that's that."

Before she could reply, the strains of a worship song began. Emma hurriedly said, "Why don't you and your family come to Gabe's after service? We're having lunch and then we're going to build a snowman," she added, grinning.

"We'd love to come!" Sheila knew the kids certainly would. She hadn't checked with Ryan, but that was okay. Like it or not, it would be good for him to be around the church family longer.

After the service, lots of people stood around talking, some praying together. This after-service mingling—being with God's family, sharing and praying for each other—was one of the real perks of church, and she loved it.

Spotting Brielle's tall, dark head, she veered over to speak with her. She wanted to tell her she was grateful that Leon had encouraged Ryan back to church.

Brielle greeted her with a hug. Ryan and Leon moved off to the side of the sanctuary.

"How's it going with you and Leon?" Sheila asked.

Brielle's lips flattened while she thought how to answer, nodding. "You know we're engaged, right?"

Sheila grinned and her brows rose. "I did not! Congratulations!"

Brielle smiled. "Thank you. That part is great. We love each other."

"But...?" Sheila prodded gently.

Brielle lowered her voice and frowned. "We've been doing financial planning. I recently inherited a lot of money and Leon wants me to invest in a startup company that he's hoping to be a partner in."

"Wow. What kind of company?"

Brielle frowned, her brows furrowing. "That's just it!" Her eyes widened. "He says he can't give me details. Yet."

"My goodness, he sounds just like Ryan!" Sheila exclaimed.

"Really?" Brielle's clear, blue-gray eyes lit with interest.

"Not about starting a business with anyone or asking me for money—we don't have any," Sheila clarified. "But the *secrecy*. He's been 'working on something' for weeks, and I should trust him and not ask questions. He won't give me any details except 'it's coming along.'"

Brielle sighed. "No wonder they're friends. They're birds of a feather."

They glanced at the men. Leon was talking while Ryan nodded, listening. Sheila was intrigued to see him looking energized, even excited, by whatever Leon was saying. She could hardly remember the last time he seemed that way at home.

Brielle continued, "I don't mind trying a new investment, but I'd like to know what I'm investing in! He says the company is preparing paperwork that has to be filed, and it has to get other legal stuff done. Then he'll tell me. He wants the partnership in place, the papers signed, from the get-go. But he needs the money to do that."

"How much does he want from you? If you don't mind my asking," Sheila said.

"He wants five thousand."

Sheila's eyes bulged.

"He's putting up fifteen, just about everything he's saved. He says the other guy is putting up twenty, and he needs to also. Based on their estimates of what's needed to get things off the ground. He thinks we'll benefit from this all our lives and that maybe he could even stop working at the base."

"Wow," Sheila said. "He must really believe in this business."

Brielle nodded. "He has a lot of confidence about it. It bothers me that he won't tell me more, though." She paused and blew out a breath. "I shouldn't talk about it, I guess. But I need prayer for wisdom."

"Are you doing marriage counseling with Mark?"

Brielle nodded. "We start in January."

"If he hasn't told you by then—if not sooner—see what Mark has to say about it."

"Has Mark helped you with Ryan?"

Sheila sighed. "He tried. But Ryan's stubborn—and not in the best of places with the Lord, if you remember."

"That's right," the other woman said. They turned thoughtfully to survey their men, still speaking earnestly a few yards away. "I wonder if they're going in on something together," she said.

Sheila said, "I wish they were. I'd feel better about it, because I know Leon's a strong believer. But if it requires capital, I don't see how Ryan could be involved. As far as I can see, we're slowly going broke as it is." She gazed at the men.

"Does Leon come home looking tired and like he's been working with his hands?"

"No, why?"

"Ryan can't jump in the shower fast enough when he gets home. I just wish I knew what he was doing to make him need it."

"If they're not in the same venture," Brielle said, "I'll bet they're still sharing notes."

The men were deep in a huddle.

"Leon really likes your husband," she continued. "Says he has a lot of good ideas."

"Like what?" Sheila asked curiously. Ryan hadn't been sharing any good ideas with her.

Brielle shrugged. "Moneymaking ones, I think. Leon's always been wanting to moonlight at something to build wealth. He's hoping to retire early, whether he stays at the base or not. Which is why he says he wants to partner in this business venture."

Sheila shook her head. "If Ryan has moneymaking ideas, I wish he'd start making some money! I'm sorry, but I hope Leon doesn't give him any thoughts of investing. He'd have to borrow the capital to do it, and I doubt very much he'd qualify right now." She thought of his being fired, and past that, his unjust criminal record. A good loan prospect, he was not.

"I'll talk to Leon about it," Brielle offered. She turned a sardonic little smile at Sheila and her eyes sparkled prettily. "Maybe he'll let something slip to give me a better idea of what he's up to."

"Yeah, and see if he knows what Ryan's up to!" Sheila said. "And remember, your money is your leverage." She felt smart to have thought of that. She wasn't the sharpest knife in the drawer and knew it. "You ought to insist on full disclosure before giving him a penny."

Brielle nodded wistfully. "You're right."

Sheila added, "I ought to insist upon no more secrets too."

"Your marriage is *your* leverage," Brielle said firmly, though eying her with sympathy.

Sheila sighed. "It ought to be." Her eyes hardened. "It *should* be." She suddenly realized she hadn't picked up the kids from Sunday school and that they were expected at Gabe's house for lunch. "I'd better get the kids and get going." With a grin she added, "We're gonna build a snowman today."

Brielle smiled, revealing perfectly white, even teeth. "That oughta be fun!" Her expression sobered and she patted Sheila's arm. "Let me just say a quick prayer for you."

Mark and Gabe had both been encouraging the congregation not to say 'I'll pray for you' and go your merry way, but to pray for one another *on the spot*. That's what being the body of Christ to one another meant. Sharing life. Sharing burdens.

Brielle prayed, "Lord, thank you for my friend, Sheila. You said that 'nothing is hidden that shall not be known,' and so I pray that whatever Ryan's doing when he leaves the house each day will come to light. I pray for healing in their marriage; healing for Ryan's hurts. We ask that you provide for this family because you promised to be our provider. Be with Sheila and bless her in Jesus' Name, Amen."

"Thank you," Sheila said. And she prayed for Brielle and Leon. She gave thanks for the coming wedding and the love that Leon and Brielle shared. She asked the Lord to give Brielle wisdom regarding the investment, for transparency on Leon's part, and that the Lord would protect the couple's finances. She prayed for the Holy Spirit to guide Leon—and Ryan —so that they'd find their way to trusting their women. "In the Mighty Name of Jesus."

They shared a heartfelt hug.

As she went to get her husband, a pang of unexpected jealousy hit. He was still in animated conversation with Leon and didn't even notice her approach until she was right next to him.

She remembered days when they used to speak together like that.

She told him they had to leave and explained about the invitation to Gabe's as they went for the kids.

Chapter Six

SNOWMAN AT GABE'S HOUSE

THEY LEFT CHURCH BENEATH a typical wintry gray sky to head to Gabe's house. Sheila and Ryan lived in a newer development right outside of Aspen Creek, so the drive through Gabe's Victorian style area with its stately older homes and charming features were relished all the more. Wide front porches, second stories with decorative lintels, long windows, and Christmas lights, wreaths, and cheery décor on most every house was festive and welcoming.

Gabe's house looked great, too, as far as holiday decorations went, which surprised Sheila, who thought bachelors didn't bother with such things. The house needed paint, but a leafless red maple in the front held strings of outdoor lights around the trunk and lower limbs, along with over-sized ornaments. A back-lit Nativity outline in front of it sparkled cheer despite the overcast sky.

More lights hung from the porch rafters and along the railing. Later she'd find out that all of it was due to Ethan, Gabe's talented and crazy generous brother, who designed sets for movies.

Soon Sheila was helping make lunch along with Emma and Tessa. Tessa Evans was the church's secretary and a friend, a tall, quiet blessing. She did everything from coordinating the pastor's meeting schedule to decorating, event planning, ordering supplies, and cooking. Sheila admired how she went about her business calmly and with never a complaint. Now and then they chatted at church, and though Tessa was quieter than some, she was an earnest believer and had a sympathetic ear.

Enjoying the camaraderie of working with other women, Sheila pushed worries about Ryan and their state of affairs to the back of her mind. But Tessa seemed quieter than usual, and Sheila hoped she'd get a chance to ask her if everything was okay.

AFTER LUNCH WHEN THEY went outdoors, she was happy to see Ryan gathering snow right along with Kacie, Jase, and Ethan for the snowman. They made two big round sections for the bottom and middle, while she helped Emma roll the head and pat it into shape. This was going to be one tall, rotund snowman.

Ethan, she noticed, while boisterous and friendly with everyone, studied Emma from time to time as if waiting for her to meet his eyes. He did it quite a lot. This was an interest, Sheila thought, that went beyond friendship. She liked Ethan very much and hoped Emma did, too. In fact, she hoped Emma liked Ethan the way he appeared to like her.

She felt more strongly than ever that Gabe wasn't right for Emma. He and Tessa hadn't even come outside, though Emma –and Ethan—seemed to love the outdoor activity.

When Gabe and the secretary eventually came out only to put on Mr. Snowman's hat, carrot nose, a scarf, and sunglasses, Sheila saw satisfaction on Tessa's face. She enjoyed being with Gabe!

Afterward, while the women and kids watched a Christmas movie, Ryan hung out in the kitchen at the table with the men. Gabe was aware of how Ryan had been unfairly fired and how he was still out of work. And she'd asked for prayer about his secrecy, so he knew about that too. Anxiously, she wondered if they would try to gently confront him and if that would raise his temper. He was so touchy about this whole situation.

Please Lord, use this time to nudge Ryan's faith. Guide the conversation so that he receives godly counsel about his behavior instead of resisting it. Encourage him somehow!

THAT EVENING, WHEN RYAN joined her in bed, she said, "Did you enjoy the time at Gabe's?"

He thought about it, putting his hands behind his head. "I did. I enjoyed seeing the kids having fun."

"Yes, that was fun." She wanted to know more. "What about when you spoke with the guys afterward? Did you have a good talk?"

"It was decent," he said. His tone intimated that this was all the details she would get. He sat up and put his arms across his chest. "I like Ethan. He's a good guy." After a pause he added, "Gabe is too, but Ethan, I don't know, he's more relatable."

Sheila breathed a sigh of relief. If he'd hated it or found the men intrusive, she'd have heard about it. But her thoughts flew back to that morning at church. "You and Leon seem like good friends," she ventured.

He nodded while saying, "Yeah, I always liked Leon. He's cool. And smart."

"Were you discussing theological things?" she asked, hoping to nudge more information from him but wanting to play it safe.

Ryan turned probing eyes to her. "No."

He was on to her. She gave up on playing it safe. "What were you talking about?"

"What kind of question is that?" His eyes narrowed.

"Any question from me leads to a fight, which is not fair, but I'd really like to know what you were discussing."

"What were you and Brielle talking about? Does it really matter?"

Sheila surveyed him sadly. He was playing cat and mouse. "Brielle said Leon wants her to invest in a startup. He wants five thousand dollars! Is this the something you've been working on?"

Ryan sighed and ran his fingers through his hair. "Brielle shouldn't have told you about their personal business. And that is *their* business, not mine."

He turned and lay down, his back to her. "Are you really going to ruin the nice day we've had by interrogating me again?"

This was escalating quickly. Sheila's stomach tightened. "Asking reasonable questions isn't an interrogation."

He turned back quickly. "It is, when I've told you before *not* to ask."

"What I hear you saying," she said, unable to keep a tremor from her voice, "is that you no longer respect our marriage covenant. Keeping secrets is not right!"

Ryan hesitated, shaking his head in the negative. The silence felt heavy. "Everyone has secrets, even in marriage. And I've made it no secret that all I'm asking from you is a little trust."

"A LITTLE?" She swallowed the lump in her throat and sat up. Her indignation rose like boiling water in a teapot. "You call disappearing all day with no explanation a LITTLE secret?"

She shook her head. "You talk about wanting my trust when you don't trust *me!* You won't trust me with the truth."

His lips compressed and he turned his head as if biting back angry words. The silence lengthened until she thought he wasn't going to respond. He turned back, but his eyes were closed, and he rubbed the bridge of his nose with one finger.

When he opened his eyes, he looked tired. "You want my trust. But I *need* yours. Needs are more important than wants."

"I need your trust too!" Pleadingly, she added, "I've always trusted you before."

He nodded and raised his head, chin down. "Then trust me now. Have patience. Things *are* shaping up. You'll be happy before Christmas, I can almost guarantee it." He turned and lay back down, facing away from her.

She sniffed and gathered her thoughts. "I will never be happy knowing you wouldn't confide in me." She turned out the light.

Trying to talk and reason with Ryan was exhausting.

THE FOLLOWING WEEK FLEW past. She and the kids baked batches and batches of cookies. They'd made thumbprints the other day. Today they were making Christmas sugar cookies with royal icing. Baking was a good way for her to carry on as though everything was hunky-dory for the kids' sakes. For her sake, too. She was doing her best to believe it would be, even after getting nowhere talking to Ryan.

Kacie and Jase ate a few cookies, and when they were cool, helped her place all but a dozen in tissue-lined dollar-store festive tins. She wrapped them with ribbon and bows and wrote out a gift tag or card to accompany each one. She spent a lot of time hand-decorating the tags and cards since the cookies weren't terribly special by themselves.

What they were was tasty and inexpensive. They showed that even in her reduced circumstances, she hadn't forgotten her friends. One tin would go to Emma and her parents, one to Pastor Mark and Maddie, one to Gabe, and one to their neighbors, the Colson's, a working, childless couple. Her mother made it clear she did not want cookies, citing health concerns for her father.

There was to be a cookie exchange hosted by the home association at the clubhouse that Friday night, but Sheila would make Buckeyes for that. It was a pricier and more time-consuming recipe, but she only needed to make two dozen for the event. Cookie exchanges were fun. She could donate twenty-four of one cookie and go home afterward with twenty-four different kinds. It made a beautiful holiday assortment for the family.

RYAN SURPRISED THEM BY coming home before dinner in an obvious good mood. He placed a bag on the table and Sheila unpacked a tin of triple-flavors of popcorn, an almond and chocolate Christmas cake, and a half gallon of Amish apple cider.

He joked with the kids and rolled around the floor with them without disappearing to take a shower first. They tried to pick his pockets of any loose change he'd gathered, all of them laughing at once. Sheila watched with full approval. She figured he *must* have started working somewhere to be this cheery.

Hopefully, he'd tell her about it.

He left to take his usual quick shower and came out, his dark hair clinging around his face in cute ringlets. She wondered, not for the first time, what kind of work made him feel the need for a shower practically the moment he walked in the door.

During dinner, he announced that he'd be home to eat with them every night for the foreseeable future. The kids were ecstatic and could hardly stop talking.

But Sheila eyed him cautiously. If it was good news, wouldn't he tell her? If he'd found a job? Having free evenings could mean he had found one, which would be cause for rejoicing, but it could also mean he wasn't working at all. How did that old song go? That freedom meant there was nothing left to lose...?

Perhaps she was just reading negative things into the situation.

On the other hand, wouldn't his secrecy make anyone wonder, if not drive them crazy? She said nothing, not wanting to rehash their recent disagreement. *Give me patience, Lord!*

After dinner, he helped her clear the table.

"You seem happy today," she said, trying to sound light-hearted. "Anything new happen?"

He set the dishes down by the sink and turned to her. "No... Just got the Christmas spirit, I guess. Anything wrong with that?"

He was on the defensive again. She couldn't ask him anything, it seemed, without making him feel that way.

He opened the dishwasher and put a few plates in. Straightening again, he turned to her. "I need to do a few things in my office. Please don't disturb me, okay?"

Sheila's lips firmed into a line. She should ask what he needed to do. She should nag him about it. Badger him to spend time with the family, for crying out loud.

She didn't want to argue. Or deal with it.

Tightly, and in a flat voice, she said "Fine."

Ryan stared at her a moment, then walked over. She thought he would put his arms around her, whisper something sweet, something reassuring. Maybe even tell her what had happened to lift his spirits, or what he needed to do upstairs. That he'd be back down soon.

He planted a kiss on her forehead and headed for the stairs.

Disappointment swept through her like a north wind. She wanted to cry.

Wait, she told herself. *Shake it off.* This was just one night. She could give him one night to hole up in his study.

EVERY NIGHT AFTER DINNER that week, he went to his office, shutting the door behind him. Not only was he living his secret life during the day, now he was doing it right in their house! By the end of the week, she got fed up and knocked on the door and tried to enter.

It was locked.

This shocked her. But why was she surprised? That locked door represented their relationship in a nutshell. Locked out. And why? Because Ryan wanted it that way.

He answered her knock by opening the door but stood across it. He didn't invite her in.

She put her hands on her hips. "May I see what you're up to?"

He pursed his lips. "Not yet."

She sighed heavily, deliberating. She was tempted to unleash all her frustration.

"A man doing things behind closed doors that he doesn't want his wife to see is not a good sign."

"I'm not doing anything I'm ashamed of. Or that you'd be ashamed of. C'mon, Sheel, you know me."

"Not anymore! You won't let me in." She motioned at the door, "You literally won't let me in!" Did he have no idea how hurtful that was?

He sighed. "It's temporary."

What should I say, Lord? Sounds from a Christmas movie on TV downstairs floated up, a discordant cheery backdrop belying the gravity of the moment. Sheila waited, knowing she needed to respond.

Ryan waited as if he knew she had more to say.

There it was. She spoke firmly. "It is not good for man to be alone." She turned and left, hoping she'd given him food for thought.

Chapter Seven

CHRISTMAS COOKING

WITH RYAN IN HIS office each night and the kids busy with toys or watching kid-appropriate holiday movies, Sheila had time to do her usual cooking ahead for Christmas dinner. The baking was done, but Christmas was a big deal, and she didn't want to miss it by laboring in the kitchen for hours, especially when she could do most of the work now.

This would enable her to spend more time with the kids as they learned how to use their new games or craft kits. She'd also have time to savor the gift of God when He sent His Son to earth.

Her plan was to prepare as much as possible and freeze or refrigerate it. The busyness in it, the bustling about the kitchen, gave her a sense of normalcy, even though her food budget wasn't normal, and her marriage felt anything but that.

About thirty-five minutes later, with her specialty "Christmas Cheesecake Pie" in the oven, she called Brielle while continuing to gather ingredients for "Grandma Rose's Red Cabbage," scalloped potatoes, and homemade macaroni and cheese. The boxed version was cheaper, but she hated to serve processed food when it could be avoided. She hadn't decided yet whether they would accompany turkey or ham, but both were usually on sale this time of year, so she wasn't worried.

Carols played softly while she waited for Brielle to pick up.

"Hey!" came her strong voice. "I was just thinking of you."

"Oh?" Sheila said. "Did you get a chance to talk to Leon?"

"I did." There was a pause. "He's doubling down on his need for secrecy, I'm sorry."

"Are you okay with that?"

"Um. No," she said. "I told him I won't contribute a penny, just like we said, unless he tells me what I'm contributing to."

"But that didn't help?"

"No. I could tell he was mad about it, but I suspect he's going to borrow the money."

Sheila shook her head. "I can't believe it isn't worth it for him to just tell you!"

"I know!"

She could imagine Brielle's large, expressive eyes at that moment.

"Honestly, I don't understand him. But I plan on letting him know that he cannot carry 'mystery' debt into our marriage. I'm not bringing any debt, and neither should he."

"I don't blame you," Sheila said. They continued to chat about other things, including the church's Christmas Eve potluck. Brielle planned on bringing a Native American Holiday Cake. She chuckled and said, "I'm of Cherokee descent but I have no idea if the cake is." She said it would include regular flour, corn flour, maple sugar and maple syrup, pumpkin, cranberries and pecans with nutmeg, cinnamon and other spices.

"That sounds very holiday-ish," Sheila said approvingly. "I can't wait to taste it! I haven't decided what to bring yet," she admitted.

"How about your savory meatballs? They are *so* good and in my opinion, better than the usual sweet and sour."

"Maybe I'll do that," Sheila said. It wasn't the cheapest dish, but weren't her church friends worth splurging for? And what did Jesus say? Doing good for the "least of these" was doing it for Him. "Yes, I'll do that, good idea," she said.

"Whatever you bring, I'm sure it will be delicious," Brielle said bracingly.

After the call, Sheila made Grandma's red cabbage. Grandma Rose, her mother's mother, had been a sociable but tough little lady whom Sheila missed very much. She was with the Lord now, but she'd left a delicious legacy behind, some of which had become traditions on holidays.

Memorial Day and July 4th saw Grandma's special potato salad on the table. Her wonderful pot roast recipe could be for any time of year. The red cabbage was a must for Thanksgiving and Christmas. It satisfied Sheila knowing she was carrying on a legacy, and that tonight's effort would be worth it on Christmas.

She thought about another tradition. Once the kids were in bed on Christmas night, she and Ryan would sit snuggled up before a crackling fire in the hearth, perhaps with a cup of eggnog or a rare glass of wine, and reflect on the day, the season, and the past year.

She wondered, would they do that this year? If Ryan hadn't come clean by then, could they, without getting testy with each other?

THE NEXT MORNING, RYAN got up at 5:30 and left the house by six. Sheila let him think she was asleep. She was too tired—and tired of his attitude—to say a word. He was en route to his 'mystery life,' as she now called it.

As she gave the kids breakfast, she fell into ruminating over their current state. He was coming home earlier as he'd promised but still disappearing into his study.

She heard him on the phone once and tried to listen through the door with every fiber of her being, but he spoke in a low voice, and she couldn't make out the words. She thought she heard 'contract.' Interesting.

Another time when she heard his muffled talking and tried to listen, she straightened guiltily when Kacie came along needing her help with something.

She cleared the table and loaded the dishwasher and found herself suddenly dreaming of the old Ryan and how things used to be. That's all she wanted—a return to the old days!

When they'd first met, he had a powerful testimony of how Christ took him from an empty life and gave him a new one. She thanked God for the two Baptist men who had approached him at a construction site one day and spoke about Jesus and why he died on a cross. They told Ryan he could be "saved" for all eternity, and that Jesus would give him a second chance at life.

Ryan wanted a second chance. Though he was innocent, he had a criminal record. And he was a father now—according to his girlfriend Candy—and that mattered. He agreed to pray with the men and then started attending church.

Candy wanted no part of it and one day got up and left. The note he found on the counter told him Kacie was his, though he had disputed that with her because Kace was born seven months after he hooked up with Candy. She said he better not even think of finding her, she was done with him and done with motherhood.

Rather than doing a paternity test or abandoning the baby, he kept her and cared for her. Fatherhood agreed with him and made him want to be a good provider. He later saw Kace's birth as a potential setback that the Lord used for good.

With his newfound faith, he surrendered a lingering bitterness about the false conviction to the Lord. That gave him the ability to forgive the men who framed him. He realized it wasn't a tragedy that was ruining his life but now saw it as a necessary step to coming to faith and a better life.

God turned something evil into something good.

Sheila liked to think Kace was his, but it didn't matter—she was theirs, now. She was hers, just as much as if she'd given birth to her.

By the time Sheila got to know Ryan, he had moved up to Blue Star, a major home building company, where he had a white-collar job managing and over-seeing blueprint specs, contracts with buyers, and interacting with suppliers. He missed working with his hands on construction projects but stuck with where the pay was higher.

It wasn't the testimony, the job, or his newfound stability that most appealed to Sheila. Those things were good—and she'd only date a fellow believer—but it was Ryan just being Ryan that won her heart.

He didn't smile a great deal back then, so when he did, she was enchanted. He had a sweet, dimpled grin that was crazy cute and changed his whole demeanor. She still loved that grin.

She loved his thick brown hair with streaks of lighter brown and tan that rippled in sunlight like waving grain. His eyes burned into her heart, deep and probing. They were alive with feeling even when he was quiet, so active in their depths that one look could send her heart swirling. It was impossible to decide what color they were. Like his hair, they changed with the light.

Before she knew him, she'd found his silence and intense eyes intimidating. He was so serious, she couldn't tell if he was a nice guy or not. It wasn't until they started speaking one night after a Bible study that she found he was a good man with a rough past. He'd opened up fairly readily and was real—you couldn't be superficial with Ryan. He disliked chit chat and found it hard to stay engaged if conversations around him were only that.

His years in construction had left him with a strong physique, muscular arms and broad shoulders. It still struck her that he had enough brawn to look intimidating but was truly gentle.

When he held or kissed her, it was like stepping into a soothing hot bath. His lovemaking was tender and unrushed, passion notwithstanding. She sighed at the thought. How she missed him! And how sad to miss someone who still slept beside her every night.

The memories continued as she collected the kids' laundry and started a load in the washing machine. He'd had an even temper —until he got fired. His anger then was deep. That frightened her. As months went by, and no company would take him on, he got depressed. That worried her. If he'd found a new job, made new friends, he'd have gotten too busy to dwell upon what happened in the past. But that hadn't happened.

Instead, he pulled back from church and, it seemed, from God.

And from her.

Recently, she'd seen remnants of the old Ryan in his better mood and seemingly more optimistic attitude. He was closer to the man he used to be.

But that man didn't keep big secrets.

Or disappear every day with no explanation. Or hide in his office with a closed door every night.

That man loved her enough to trust her with the truth.

She gave the kitchen floor a quick mop and went to remind the kids that Grandma was coming to watch them.

SHE FOUND KACE AND Jase cross-legged on the rug before the Christmas tree, staring at the lights as if mesmerized. "What're you guys doing?"

Kacie broke her gaze from the tree. "We're dreaming of Christmas."

Sheila surveyed them. "If you want to dream about Christmas, why not stare at the Nativity?" She pointed to theirs atop the mantel of the fireplace, nestled among faux greenery. "You have to look at Jesus to know what Christmas is about."

Kacie said, "I know, Mom. But the presents come under the tree! We're imagining the presents we'll get!"

"Yeah!" echoed Jase.

Sheila stifled a laugh. "Jesus is the best present you could get. Ever."

Jase's face fell. "But we ARE gonna get presents, right, Mom?"

She kissed the top of their heads. "Of course you are."

Her mother arrived and Sheila left to do her weekly stop at the church's common room for groceries. The food came from local restaurants and bulk food services whose items were close to expiration or sometimes past it. It was surplus food, and a blessing that they donated it. She never knew what would be in stock in a given week and sometimes there were nice surprises.

She hadn't planned on taking a detour but impulsively drove out of town, passing the snow-covered hills of the countryside. Miles of fields blanketed in white, dotted here and there with farmsteads, silos, barns and cows, was so peaceful. She played Christmas carol CDs—their car was old enough to have a player, thankfully—and sang along to Jesus at the top of her lungs.

She could just see Him smiling at her sometimes-croaky voice, but she was sure He welcomed her worship, no matter the vocal deficiency. Jesus accepted those who came to Him as they were, and everyone could please Him with praise.

She contemplated His nearness. How awesome it was that He promised to be with her always. But that reminded her of her prayer needs. Of Ryan and his secrets.

Her mood plummeted. Just like that, worries about him, their bills, and their future began edging out her joy like a silent rising tide smothering green growth on a riverbank.

Aloud she said, "Sorry, Lord." And headed toward Grace Church.

Chapter Eight

ANOTHER CARING FRIEND

SHEILA COULD SEE THE comforting steeple of the Church in the distance but couldn't get her husband off her mind. She could sometimes turn off the worries when she was busy with the kids and the house, but when she was alone like now in the car, they flew at her like a noisy flock of birds coming to roost.

These days, it seemed those birds were pecking at her feet, always right under the surface of her life, just waiting to pop out and ruin her day. She'd be going along like a clear stream, bubbling with a "life is good" attitude around the kids, but then she'd get alone and her less cheery thoughts would churn up like silt, muddying the waters.

She pulled into the church parking lot, turned off the engine and headed for the doors. If Tessa was in her office, she'd stop and see her. And talk about anything, anything at all—except Ryan and their situation. It would take her mind off it. And why ruin someone else's day?

Seeing the glow of lights in the dim hallway coming from the secretary's office, Sheila knocked and peeked inside. Tessa invited her in warmly.

The soft shimmer of sparkling lights running along ivy and holly vines on Tessa's desk and bookshelves met her eyes. Other holiday décor, understated and elegant, greeted her as well. The old-fashioned mantel over a huge fireplace sported more lights, and Tessa's lovely old-world style nativity, a family heirloom that Sheila remembered from past years, sat on a sturdy wooden file cabinet.

Tessa's decorating was always picture-perfect, and their old church building had the architectural character that shone beneath her touch. There were few square or plain rectangular walls or rooms in the building. Instead, most had domed entranceways, nooks, built-in shelving, wooden wainscot, roomy closets, rooms within rooms within rooms, and other 19th century features. The sanctuary was huge, with a domed ceiling that had beautiful stained glass running along eight lines of heavy wooden beams.

The church hadn't been able to afford a modern building. Ryan, with his knowledge of construction, had told her what a blessing it was for them to get this one on auction at a fraction of its market value.

After initial greetings, Tessa gently asked how Sheila was doing.

The secretary knew Ryan's history, how he got fired, and that he'd been missing church. Sheila had intended not to say a word or be negative. But from the moment she opened her mouth, her worries spilled out. Having a sympathetic listener was like a welcome mat for the troubling thoughts and they flew out like hornets disturbed from their nest.

"He hasn't found a new job that I know of, though he still leaves the house every morning as if he has one. He still won't tell me anything, and he spends most evenings holed up in his study. Which is locked."

Tessa frowned. "That's troubling. What do you think he's up to?" she asked gently.

Sheila's brows furrowed and her lips flattened. "I have no idea. I wish it were job-hunting. He says he's working on *something,* but it will be a surprise. I get no details, but he's out early and comes home late. He hardly sees the kids. Also, he says he doesn't want to be someone's *hire*. That tells me he's not even looking for a job!"

Tessa interjected, "I was glad to see him at Gabe's that day."

"Yes," Sheila acknowledged. "I was glad too, believe me."

"What do you think he's doing?" Tessa asked. She came around her desk and leaned against it, giving Sheila her undivided attention.

Sheila shook her head. "I don't know. I *pray* he isn't getting into trouble. Or back into...you know, drugs, or bad company." She felt guilty for saying that. Ryan had never been a user but somehow people got the impression he was. She didn't like to talk about his having been framed for dealing, so she let people think what they wanted.

She added, "Well, not drugs. He was never a drug addict or anything, you know."

Suddenly she wondered if Ryan might have gone into dealing drugs for real. He'd been framed for it, and he knew there was a lot of money in it.

Her logical mind argued. He despised drug dealers. No, he would never do that. He *was* a Christian! He answered to God. He'd just lost his way for a while.

She looked pleadingly at Tessa. "Please pray for him."

"I have been!" Tessa assured her. Gently she asked, "Are you managing to get by? Financially?"

That might have seemed too personal a question coming from just anybody, but Sheila knew Tessa was asking on behalf of the church.

Pastor Mark had approached Sheila one Sunday about accepting help from the church's benevolence fund, but she'd refused. Her family shouldn't be a charity case unless they were down to their last cent. Bad enough she was using the common room food pantry every week. She wouldn't take financial help unless they were starving.

"Well, I'm here to see what groceries are in the common room," she admitted, embarrassed even though everyone at Grace Church was encouraged to take advantage of what the church received each week from area businesses.

She added, "I think we've pretty much exhausted our savings." She wanted Tessa to know she was only there because her family needed help. As soon as she said it, she realized that was her pride speaking.

Ryan said they were still okay. They were paying their bills.

She ought to check their accounts and see for herself. Why hadn't she?

She was too afraid of how sadly changed their finances were. Her statement was true enough. They'd been drawing on their savings for almost a year. How could it not be near depletion after all this time with no income?

She readjusted her handbag over one shoulder. "I guess I should get home. I've been out for two hours and my mom's watching the kids."

Tessa thanked her, but her face was drawn. The secretary was never a bundle of joy, but this looked more serious. She asked, "How are *you* doing?"

Tessa shook her head in the negative but said, "I'm fine."

Sheila asked a few questions and discovered that Tessa was sweet on Gabe, their pastor-in-training. Gabe, who was planning to propose to Emma.

She'd suspected as much. With a little grin, she said, "You know, you and Gabe are a lot alike."

"I think so, too!" She rubbed her arms and went back to her seat at the desk.

Sheila cautiously shared her thoughts about Gabe not being right for Emma, and Tessa agreed wholeheartedly. Sheila said Gabe's brother Ethan who was visiting for the season, seemed exactly right for Emma, and Tessa agreed again.

This was a subject she probably should not have spoken about since Emma wasn't there. But it seemed to fill Tessa with hope, and Sheila had told Emma what she thought about her and Gabe. She wasn't saying anything she hadn't said to her face.

Still, she had to watch her words. It was all too easy to say negative things about the people you most loved!

Tessa asked if Emma felt the same way.

"She agrees with me more than she wants to admit. Which is what worries me. She doesn't want to hurt Gabe, but I don't want to see her make a mistake that will affect the rest of her life."

Tessa bit her lip. "I worry for Gabe, for the same reason."

A little smile curled the edges of Sheila's mouth. "I thought you might."

Tessa added, "If Emma could make him happy, I'd be able to live with whatever happens. But I don't think she can." She looked sadly at Sheila. "I'm thinking of getting a new job."

Sheila's heart lurched. Tessa was so important to the church. And was a friend she would miss if she left. "Oh, no! Don't do that."

Tessa frowned. "I don't want to, but it's better than wishing I had a guy who's taken. It's not spiritually healthy for me to stay."

Troubled, Sheila surveyed her. "Please don't be hasty. They're not engaged. There's still hope."

Tessa sighed. "Gabe had me help him pick an engagement ring for her."

Sheila's eyes widened. "He didn't!"

Tessa nodded and her lips hardened. "Don't tell Emma. He wants to surprise her."

Men and their surprises! Secrets, convenient secrets. And how obtuse of Gabe to ask Tessa to do that when even she could see the secretary cared for him.

"I'll pray for you," she said sincerely. "Sorry, but I have to go. My mom will be wondering what happened to me." With one hand on the door handle, she stopped and turned. "She thinks I'm at the grocery store. I didn't mention I was coming here—she blames Ryan."

Tessa said, "Thanks for stopping in. Please don't say anything about my leaving. Even if Emma turns Gabe down, it doesn't mean he'll suddenly look at me differently."

Sheila gave her a compassionate look. "We have to pray that the Lord has His way. In all our lives."

If she could only trust in that herself.

Chapter Nine

A Word from the Lord

SHELIA BROUGHT THE GROCERIES from the food pantry to the car, thanking God for the provisions. After shutting the trunk firmly, she sat with the engine on, letting it warm. She rubbed her gloved hands together and sighed. A cloud of condensation left her lungs.

That noisy flock of birds was coming at her again.

One minute she felt encouraged due to the groceries and from sharing her burdens. The next minute, she felt their weight all over again and was fretting.

Talking about problems could be therapeutic, but it could also magnify the weight of them. Even talking to God did that because she was prone to give Him her troubles but then take them right back. Still...

Pray. That's what she ought to do.

She prayed for Tessa, who was ready to quit because she couldn't conquer her attraction to Gabe. For Emma, expecting Gabe to propose on Christmas Eve but not wanting to admit he wasn't the right man for her.

She prayed for Ryan. That she could see him with compassion the way God did. Not just with censure and worry. Just thinking about it made her insides tight. She was almost ready to cry. It seemed pointless to pray because her prayers hadn't been answered before. She'd asked God to make Ryan be honest with her yet he still wasn't.

Nevertheless, she thought of her mother's attitude about him and prayed her parents would be merciful to him and give him the benefit of the doubt.

But you're not doing that.

Sheila froze. The thought was not hers but was dropped into her mind.

And it was true. Utterly and absolutely. She was fretting and wondering and worrying, not giving Ryan the benefit of the doubt. And certainly not trusting God.

God, the Almighty God of heaven and earth who had called every created thing into being with the words of His mouth and His mighty power. The God who cared so much for her—and Ryan, and their kids—that He had come down and walked among them and died on the cross for them.

Christmas was less than two weeks away, the time to remember His coming, and she hadn't been remembering it at all.

Someone once said that Christians who lived as if God isn't God were "practical atheists." She believed in God and His power. She believed He could take care of them. She believed He could take care of Ryan.

But she wasn't living like she did.

Aloud she said, "You're right, Lord. I haven't been doing that. If I trusted You more to take care of our family, and Ryan—and our marriage—I wouldn't be wallowing in doubt and fear. Or anxiety."

"Help me to really trust that You're working in Ryan and through everything that's happened. Help me to give him the benefit of the doubt!"

"You give me so much—forgiveness and love, when I don't deserve them. And you *don't* give me the wrath of God that my sins do deserve, because of Jesus's finished work on the cross. Thank you for pouring out your love through your Son."

She lowered her head into her hands, leaning over the steering wheel. More. There was more she had to confess.

"I've been resenting Ryan for not giving me what I feel I deserve. I surrender that to You, Lord. Here and now. Help me to trust that he's doing the best he can, that he's going to provide just as he says, because *You're* going to provide."

She felt a sudden sense of the presence of the Lord. Her heart burst with the awareness; how amazing to serve a God who came down, a God who showed up, a God who cared.

"Lord, grant me your Spirit so I might always be aware of Your presence. So that I *will* trust You and stop obsessing over what's *wrong* in my life."

It was easy to pray that. She wanted to trust Him. Why was it so difficult to do?

Tears surfaced and made a cold trail on her cheeks. She sat up and wiped them with a gloved hand. As she drove home, she determined, from that day forward, to act like a believer and *trust the Lord*.

She supposed that meant trusting Ryan too. Giving him the benefit of the doubt. The Lord wouldn't have nudged her to do so if He didn't know she was safe to do it. Ryan promised numerous times that they were okay and things would improve. She ought to believe him unless he proved otherwise.

As she considered how this would change her attitude and words, how she would behave more lovingly, it reminded her of the old days, the old Ryan, when love between them wasn't strained. The sweet, affectionate man he was. The closet jokester.

The night he proposed came to mind, as crisp and clear as if it were yesterday.

They'd been out to a movie and an expensive dinner, and he'd taken her home and come inside. It was early January, and her family's Christmas tree still sparkled warmly in a corner of the room. Snow was falling lightly outside.

Her parents were elsewhere in the house. Her little brother was up in his room. Ryan had said he wanted to talk – that was a clue that something big was up, because he rarely said anything of the sort. He moved toward her on the sofa and took her hands in his. He had that sexy shadow covering his jaw and chin, masculine and handsome. His serious eyes, filled with love, stared into hers.

He leaned toward her and said earnestly, "I love you so much!"

"I love you too!" she replied.

"I don't just love you," he returned. "I am *crazy* in love with you. I need you."

"I need you too!" Never a word wizard, that was the best she could do with her heart pounding like mad. She suspected what was coming and felt ready to jump out of her skin. No, better, into his arms!

He said, "I hope you do, because I want you to be mine forever." With one hand, he gently moved some stray hair off her face. He pulled out a small jewelry box and opened it and held it out to her. A beautiful diamond ring sparkled out at her, its facets twinkling with colors in the light like prisms.

"Will you marry me, Sheel? Will you be mine?"

Her heart was already full, soft as fresh snow, but now it melted like butter that must surely be settling in a pool around her feet.

"You know I will! I want to, yes!"

Ryan's eyes lit with joy. Smiling, he took out the ring and placed it on her finger. He kissed her quickly, took a peek to ensure they were still alone and then drew her close and held her against him.

"Thank you," he whispered in her ear. Then, drawing back, his lips went over hers and he took her in his arms and kissed her with a slow, lingering kiss. Her body felt shivery and tingly, and she loved every second of that closeness. The whole world felt good and warm and right. She returned the kiss eagerly.

They were so in love.

Ryan could still make her shiver with pleasure when he sometimes came up behind her and put his arms around her middle and snuggled his lips against her neck.

If the kids saw them like that, especially Jase, he'd rush over and grab their legs, barging in on the intimacy as if he felt left out.

Those scenes didn't happen lately.

She sighed. She wanted that closeness back again. Maybe it would have to start with her. Maybe it would start if she was able to trust, to give him the benefit of the doubt the way she wished her folks would.

The Lord said she wasn't doing that.

That would have to change.

Chapter Ten

THE HENDERSONS MAKE AN OFFER

BEFORE GOING HOME—SHE TEXTED her mother to make sure it was okay—Sheila headed toward Main Street for a chance to pick up a few things still needed for Christmas. She would pop into Snowberry Pharmacy first, as the kids needed shampoo and she needed dental floss. Snowberry was more like a general store than a pharmacy, and prices were no higher than at the Village Grocery. Plus, it was less crowded.

While there, she'd look for inexpensive items that could double as stocking stuffers. Like hair clips for Kacie, a set of erasable markers for Jase, and new toothbrushes. Something inexpensive for Ryan too.

She passed Amy's Amish Quilts and thought of the box of chocolates she still hadn't purchased and wasn't sure she would. They were so good—but so pricey. This wasn't a year for splurging. She passed the shop without going in.

When she got home, the kids came charging up from the basement followed by Mrs. Henderson, wiping her hands of chalk. "We've been coloring on the boards," she explained.

"We drew a Christmas tree and presents, and—and a star!" shouted Jase.

"The Star of Bethlehem," added Kacie, proudly.

"Oooh, I want to see it!" Sheila said, giving them each a quick hug and kiss. Mrs. Henderson followed her into the kitchen.

Putting the food away, Sheila was happy that this week there was plenty of frozen chicken, fresh broccoli crowns, and heavy cream—she hadn't seen cream in the food pantry before but could use it to make ice cream. There was frozen sugar cookie dough—the kind with a blue-winged angel in the center of each slice. It wasn't the healthiest option for her family, but it was Christmas time. A few extra treats wouldn't hurt them.

"Oh, your friend Emma came by and dropped these off," her mother said, showing her a festive plate of chocolate-covered star cookies wrapped in cellophane and topped with a bow. It was Mrs. Dawson's Christmas specialty cookie and Sheila's whole family loved them.

"I wish I hadn't missed Emma!" she cried. Visits from her friend were infrequent and only because Emma's hours had been cut, was she able to come by, Sheila was sure.

"Did you give her our cookie present?" she asked.

Mrs. Henderson nodded. "Kacie did. She was very excited."

"Good." She returned to the groceries to put them away. Uncomfortable under her mother's prying eyes, she said, "Mom, could you see that the kids clean up downstairs? Then we can talk." She smiled, hoping to soften her words.

Mrs. Henderson glanced plaintively at the groceries, but said, "Sure."

Sheila hurriedly put away the rest, thankful her mom wasn't watching.

Afterward, with a few free minutes, she went to the kitchen nook with the desk holding her laptop. She'd check email and maybe Facebook. But the kids were suddenly there at her side.

"Mom, come look at what we drew!" Kacie said.

"You said you would look!" Jase pleaded, grasping her hand.

She let him lead her downstairs where most of their toys and games were. A large whiteboard hung on one wall, and an equally large old-fashioned blackboard—Ryan had found it at a yard sale—hung beside it.

Both were sprinkled with holiday drawings, the blackboard in chalk, and the whiteboard with dry-erase marker. Her mother was a bit of an artist and enjoyed teaching the kids basic drawing methods. Jase's creations were still very childish, but advanced for a four-year-old. At least, Sheila thought so.

She saw the big Star of Bethlehem, and that her mother had added a stable underneath it replete with the holy family and a cow. Kacie had drawn rolling hills and two shepherds in the background. Jase had added a wild forefront of grass in a frenzy of wide strokes, and to the side, he'd drawn a recognizable Christmas tree with presents.

She gushed over the drawings and was happy to add a fluffy sheep near the stable when the kids urged her to help. Mrs. Henderson added halos to Joseph, Mary and baby Jesus, and then had Kacie help her draw an angel hovering over the scene.

"Don't!" Jase cried, when his grandmother picked up the eraser and would have started to wipe the whiteboard clean.

"Yeah! Let's keep it here until Daddy sees it," added Kacie.

"Let's keep it until Christmas!" shouted Jase.

Mrs. Henderson looked questioningly at Sheila, who nodded. "Let's keep it until Christmas at least." She got a joyful hug around her legs from Jase.

She made the kids take a bath, as there was just as much chalk on their hands and faces as the blackboard.

Her mother followed her into the kitchen as she washed her hands and started gathering things for dinner. Her mother washed her hands and then turned to Sheila while drying them with a kitchen towel. "I have a proposition."

A warning light flicked on inside Sheila. Was this about that loan again? She hadn't had a chance to check their accounts. Truthfully, she hadn't wanted to. She didn't want to see how they were slowly losing everything they'd saved, or how bad off they probably were. She didn't want more reason to believe Ryan was failing them.

All she wanted to know was, what was going on with him and Leon.

Mrs. Henderson continued, "Ryan enjoyed working in construction, didn't he? I mean, building? And renovating?" She glanced around at the impressive kitchen.

Sheila nodded. She had hoped he would return to that field of work, even if it meant doing the manual labor of construction again. He enjoyed working with his hands, and it was certainly better than not working.

"Well, your father and I need a few projects done on the house. We'd like the back porch to get screened in."

"Is that a winter job?" Sheila asked.

"Well, no, but our bathroom needs new cabinets installed, the living room could use some updates, and I'm sure we could come up with other things he could do for us indoors."

Sheila nodded thoughtfully. "He might like that."

Mrs. Henderson frowned. "Might? He needs work and this is work. We'll pay him well."

Sheila shook her head. "I know, but he's busy with whatever he's doing."

Her mother put her hands on her hips. "Has he brought home a paycheck yet?"

Sheila swallowed. She should have checked their accounts. Still, she had no reason to think Ryan had made any money and told her mother she didn't think so.

Mrs. Henderson came closer. Lowering her voice she asked, "Have you considered following him when he leaves the house in the morning?"

A well of objections rose in Sheila's throat. It was an appalling idea. "I have the kids at home when he leaves!"

"What about having someone else follow him? There are private detectives for that."

Sheila frowned. "Mom, that takes money, and I wouldn't do that to Ryan."

Her mother put her hands on her hips and her eyes hardened. "Under the circumstances, don't you think it's warranted?"

Sheila took lettuce out of the fridge and started tearing it up for a salad with such zeal it was good she wasn't brushing Kace's hair instead.

She thought how to answer. Turning back to her mother she said. "It would be a mistake. Ryan wants me to trust him. If he found out I was following him or having him followed, it would destroy our marriage."

Her mother huffed out air. "Bah! His behavior is already doing that." She shook her head and then planted a quick kiss on Sheila's cheek. "I'll see you next time. If you change your mind, your father and I could follow him or hire someone to do it."

"Don't, Mom!" Sheila cried. "He'll think I put you up to it. Just don't, okay?"

Her mother threw up her hands, lips pursed. "Fine. Have it your way."

Chapter Eleven

The Offer is Refused

At dinner that night, Sheila was anxious to tell Ryan about her parents' job offer but would wait until they were alone. She knew that anything having to do with working was a touchy subject for him and could end up in an argument. He hadn't used to be so fragile.

Fragile. That was a word she had never associated with her big, strong husband before. But emotionally, at least for the time being, it seemed true. She had to tiptoe around him when it came to wanting her questions answered or mentioning anything about his unemployment.

After dinner, when Ryan stayed downstairs instead of disappearing into his office, Sheila felt like yelling 'hallelujah!' She wanted to ask him why, what had changed, but decided that sometimes silence was indeed golden. It was all part and parcel of her new trust in the Lord, her resolve not to take back the worries of their lives.

She made hot chocolate and the family sat in the living room to drink it. Kace picked up a book and Jase put on a video game.

She loved sipping a hot drink and basking in the cheery lights of the Christmas tree and the special décor she pulled out for the season. Having Ryan near her made it even more special.

She remembered her mother's job offer. Since Ryan merely had to turn it down if he wasn't interested, she decided it was safe enough to bring it up. She wasn't going to insist he take it or rant and rave if he didn't. And it wasn't something the kids couldn't hear about.

She dove in. "Honey, my mother mentioned that they need some work done around the house. Like getting cabinets installed and other small renovations. She wants to know if you'd let them hire you."

He nodded thoughtfully.

"She knows you do good work," Sheila added, hoping to encourage him.

He was still nodding and thinking. "I can't say I'm eager to work for your parents."

"I know," Sheila understood why.

"But they are my in-laws," he continued. "So I can try to help them out. In a month or so."

"You can't start now?" she asked, instantly regretting it. He would probably think she was fishing for information again.

His mouth twisted while again he thought how to answer. "No, I can't start now." He gave her a look that was almost reproving but tinged with—amusement? He wasn't angry or defensive! She felt things must be looking up for him to react this way—something good like a new job prospect, maybe?

Her heart swelled with relief. If he was confident, it gave her confidence. It emboldened her to ask, "And you're going to tell me why, right?" she coaxed.

He inched closer to her on the sofa, removed the hot chocolate from her hands and put it on a side table. He put his arms around her and drew her close. Sheila settled against him, snuggling into his warmth. This was more like it! She twined her arms around his neck.

Kace looked up and giggled. Smiling, she returned to her book.

"Yes, I'm going to tell you about it soon."

Soon. That dreaded word. A host of objections flew to her lips but she remained silent. She had to give him the benefit of the doubt. The same as she wished her parents would give him. She wanted to show God that she could give him that. But there was no harm in asking the next question, was there?

Softly, she said, "Don't you think we could use the money? It's almost Christmas."

He breathed in deeply, his chest expanding against her. "We're still okay. And I have a Christmas surprise for you. Don't. Worry." He kissed the side of her face. "I'll tell you everything soon." He rubbed her arms and sat back to take a sip of his chocolate.

Many more arguments rose up in Sheila's head. He was being unfair. He wasn't trusting her. He wasn't being honest. They were married and supposed to be one flesh. How would he feel if he was in her place? He'd said she would find out before Christmas, and it was fast approaching.

He reached for her hand with one of his and squeezed it. She didn't want to ruin the moment or his mood. She didn't want to argue. He really didn't deserve the benefit of the doubt, but she was committed to giving it. God was like that with His people. With her.

She said only, "And this secrecy is absolutely necessary until then?"

He didn't answer right away. Then, leaning to speak in her ear, whispered, "For me, it is."

IN THE MIDDLE OF the night, Tessa called with grave news. Ethan had been in a car accident and was in the hospital getting evaluated. They already determined he had multiple bone breaks and that his head had been gashed by glass. Various tests would tell them more.

She and Ryan held hands and prayed for him immediately. She prayed for Emma, knowing she cared so much for Ethan, and for Gabe, his brother, who must be full of worries.

To everyone's relief, they'd learned by the next day that Ethan was expected to make a full recovery. Sheila could imagine the collective sigh of relief from the church body.

Emma was with Gabe and couldn't talk much when Sheila called, but she could tell how relieved her friend was. She hoped that Ethan's close call would nudge Emma into seeing that she had strong feelings for him. And not as strong for Gabe. The man deserved to know.

And Tessa wouldn't have to quit her job, she couldn't help thinking.

She loved Emma dearly, but the poor girl was making a mess of things.

THAT SUNDAY, SHEILA WAS encouraged when Ryan came to church again. She noticed Pastor Mark taking him aside before the service, and that filled her with hope. She hoped he would ask him about how things were going, and if he'd found work, and by the way, had he told Sheila what he was up to?

One of the functions of the church was to hold people accountable for non-Christian behavior. She had reminded Mark about their difficulties after running into him on one of her common room food pantry visits. She told him she had promised God to trust Him in everything but that she still struggled from time to time.

"Do you want to have peace?" he asked, eyeing her gently.

"I do."

"Give up trying to control Ryan. Trying to coerce him into talking. Give him to the Lord. Trust him to the Lord. He promises to give us a supernatural peace if we commit our problems and cares to Him. As Isaiah said, He will keep 'in perfect peace' those who are steadfast because they trust in Him. And Paul tells us in Philippians, 'Be anxious for nothing, but in everything, by prayer and petition, with thanksgiving, present your requests to God. And the peace of God, which surpasses all understanding, will guard your hearts and your minds in Christ Jesus.'"

Sheila said, "I am trusting God more than I was before."

Pastor Mark nodded. "That's good. Here, let me pray for you to trust Him completely." He took her hand and patted it, then held it while he prayed.

He prayed for a good job for Ryan, for him to follow Jesus closely, and for transparency in their marriage. He prayed that Sheila would remember God's ways were past finding out, but that He always had our best in mind. He asked that she receive a great blessing for putting Ryan into His hands, and leaving her anxieties at the foot of the Cross. "Let it be a blessing beyond anything she could ask or think," he said.

He gave her a warm hug. "I appreciate you, Sheila. Maddie and I both do. We've seen your steadfast faith all these months and I can assure you, the Lord sees it too. Remember, 'He is a rewarder of them that diligently seek Him.'"

Sheila nodded, "Thank you. Thank you for the reminders."

"Thanks for stopping to talk. I look forward to seeing you and Ryan and the kids at church."

"Do you think you could talk to him again?" she asked.

He nodded. "I'll do that."

She figured he was doing that now. He gave Ryan a pat on the back while she watched, and the men shook hands. She looked away hurriedly so Ryan wouldn't think she was spying on him. Though she was, sort of.

Chapter Twelve

DISCOVERY ON MAIN STREET

WHATEVER MARK SAID TO Ryan at church was a mystery to Sheila because he didn't say a word about it. She decided not to mention it either. She didn't want him thinking she'd put Mark up to it. Even though she had.

On Monday, Ryan left the house early, as usual. Sheila was planning to run into town for Ryan's favorite flavored coffee, Holiday Grog, at Village Grocery. And for that box of Amish chocolates. What had she been thinking? She couldn't stop the tradition. Ryan and the children loved the Amish treats, and she did, too.

The ladies made them by hand starting in October and always sold out. People came from far and wide to get them. Sheila prayed there would be one box left.

Why had she put this off until five days before Christmas? She ought to have come to her senses sooner. She'd bought a box every year since their first Christmas as newlyweds.

No, actually, Ryan started the tradition. But she kept it up. The chocolates were the traditional accompaniment to her pumpkin pie. It *was* a splurge but it was worth it for Christmas.

She grabbed the kids and left the house right after breakfast, hoping to beat the holiday crowd. As they drove to Main Street, Jase squealed at the more exciting Christmas displays, their lights cheering up the overcast day.

"Look, Mommy, look!" or "Kace, look!" was the backseat refrain.

Minutes later they were in the store, bustling despite the early hour. Sheila looked in the usual places where boxes of the goodies were normally displayed. There were other baked goods, plenty of pies, rolls and muffins, but no specialty chocolates.

With a sinking heart, she joined the line at the register to ask Amy about it—just in case she'd missed them. Amy and Sunshine were easy to tell apart from a distance because Amy, married and older, wore a white headcap, while Sunshine, still single, wore black. They called it a "covering."

They both wore long dark blue or black dresses with a cape over the bodice and a white apron from the waist down. Today, Sheila noticed, Amy wore a pretty but sedate purple dress. Purple was traditionally a color for royalty, so she figured the new color was in honor of the season for King Jesus.

The kids were excited to look at all the cellophane wrapped goodies, but Sheila cautioned them to stay close. Lots of strangers frequented the shops at this time of year. One could never be too careful.

There was a good number of people ahead of her, and Sheila resigned herself to a long wait. She spotted Sunshine, also in the pretty purple, coming out briskly from the back of the store with a customer. She saw Sheila and her face lit with a big smile.

As she got close, she exclaimed, "I thought you forgot us this year! I was wondering when you'd come around."

Sheila gave her a pleading look. "Am I too late? I don't see any left."

"Oh, we saved you one!" she practically sang.

The customer thanked her for her help and continued toward the exit.

Sunshine drew closer and whispered, "C'mon!" She motioned toward the back of the store. Grabbing Kace and Jace by the hand, Sheila followed.

Glancing at the kids, Sunshine gushed, "Look how big you two are getting!"

"I'm four!" Jase volunteered.

"I'm seven!" Kacie said proudly.

"My goodness! Soon you'll be older than me!" She winked and they giggled.

At the back of the store was another counter with a register. Sunshine went behind it and pulled out a one-pound gold colored box of chocolates, replete with a red ribbon tied in a neat bow. A sticky note on it said, "Sheila Preston."

"Merry Christmas," she said, smiling widely as she held it out.

"I can't believe you did this for us," Sheila said, staring down at the box. She met Sunshine's merry eyes. That woman was always happy. "I can't thank you enough!" She fished in her purse for her credit card, but to her astonishment Sunshine said gently, "No, this is our gift for you this year."

The plump woman leaned in and whispered. "Mom got ear of your husband's troubles. You've been a faithful customer for a long time. You've bought plenty from us over the years. It's the least we could do."

Sheila was so touched she hardly knew what to say. She felt downright teary. "I have to give you a hug!" She hurried to round the counter.

Sunshine met her halfway. "I'll take that hug, thank you!" She looked down at the kids. "What about you two? Don't I get a hug?"

They grinned sheepishly, but first Kace, and then Jase obediently gave her one. They broke out into wider grins as they were hugged in turn.

"Well, that was worth a box of chocolates any day!" Sunshine beamed, smiling from ear to ear as if the Prestons had made her day.

"Merry Christmas," Kacie added.

"Merry Christmas indeed!" Sunshine cried.

"Thank you so much," Sheila said again. "This was so kind. God bless your Christmas!"

"He already has," Sunshine assured her.

As they left the shop, Sheila held up her box of chocolates so that Amy, behind the register, saw it and gave her a big smile. "Thank you!" Sheila cried.

"Merry Christmas!" Amy called in reply, smiling. Small gray curls peeked out from the cap around her face. The rest of her hair, Sheila knew, was in a bun under it. Amish women didn't cut their hair.

That 16 oz box of chocolates may as well have been a grand prize ticket at a fair. That's how blessed Sheila felt.

She had failed to get it early, but God hadn't failed to provide!

As THEY HEADED HOME, Sheila stopped for a red light, still basking in the glow of Amy and Sunshine's kindness. Her eyes roamed the festive street—and she nearly did a double take—Ryan! With Leon!

No sooner than she saw them, they disappeared into a run-down building right next to Maple & Main, the café she and Emma often ate at. Her heart thumped. Why would they enter that old building? She couldn't remember the last time it had an occupant. It was the kind of place you hardly saw and just looked past at all the more appealing storefronts and shops. In truth, she'd hardly known it was there.

The kids hadn't seen their dad, or they would have said something.

All the joy from the Amish ladies dissipated in a cloud of worries as her thoughts churned like a swirling dust devil. What were he and Leon up to? The idea of something bad, something illegal even, played at the edges of her mind.

Wouldn't that explain why he was pulling away from her? He was ashamed and didn't want to get caught. Why else wouldn't he want her to know about it?

She was tempted to park and go after them, but she'd have to bring the kids. She wished she could go and demand to know what they were doing. She was so taken aback and distracted that the driver behind her had to beep when the light turned green and her car hadn't moved.

She drove on, her mind still reeling and so absorbed in wondering and worrying, she went right past Village Grocery's main entrance drive. She caught herself in time to turn left at the corner and pull into the store's side entry parking lot.

She turned off the engine and sat in the car ruminating. Ryan was with Leon. *Good.* But it was a weekday—didn't Leon work at the air force base? Maybe he had days off for Christmas. She sat there drumming her fingers on the steering wheel, still wondering whether she ought to go back and see what they were up to.

Was this proof that Brielle was right? And the men were in on something together?

"Mom, I'm cold," Kacie complained from behind her.

"My nose is cold," Jase added.

"Oh, I'm sorry! Let's go." She got out and herded the kids into the store, but her mind was still fixated on what the men were doing in that building. She ought not to jump to conclusions that it was anything underhanded. But didn't drug addicts use old, abandoned buildings? Even here in Aspen Creek?

Her rational mind slowly took over as she grabbed a cart in the store. *Ryan would never resort to such a thing. He wouldn't do anything illegal. He was a Christian, even if not in the best of places right now.* Yes, she was sure of that. Leon, she felt, wouldn't either.

But they were up to something. They'd gone in purposefully, without hesitation. If she went after them now, she could catch them red-handed, whatever they were doing. Ryan would *have* to explain it to her, then.

She checked her list and noticed just in time when the kids disappeared down the aisle with small toys. "Hey, stay with me, you guys!" she called. As they trudged back with long faces, she imagined the confrontation with Ryan. He'd explain things, but he'd probably be furious.

To him, her following them would be absolute proof that she didn't trust him.

But she'd asked God to reveal what was going on. What if this was that? Was she supposed to follow up? Go in after them?

Ironically, she remembered something Ryan had said once. Something like, *Trust means not needing to know. If you trusted me, you wouldn't have to be worried or anxious.*

That sounded a lot like something God would say! Was He saying that to her now? How could he use Ryan, in his sorry spiritual state, to correct *her*? It didn't seem fair.

But somehow she felt that was the case. The Lord required trust even when His people couldn't understand difficult circumstances. This was no different. It was a faith test. She had promised to trust Him, and to give Ryan the benefit of the doubt.

She found the ingredients she needed, grabbed kids, and they headed to the checkout.

Okay. She would *not* go after them. She might, however, ask Ryan later why he and Leon had gone into that abandoned building. He always said she'd find out what he was up to before Christmas, and for goodness sakes, it was days away!

It was past time she knew.

But a sinking feeling hovered about her heart. Something wasn't right. As she got Jase and Kacie buckled and then settled in her seat for the ride home, she searched her mind and her heart for the issue. Confronting Ryan was not something she relished doing. Was that it?

There. It was as if the Holy Spirit was whispering again, *Wait and trust. Trust Me.*

She loved that God cared enough to infuse her thoughts. She would do her best to obey and trust.

But now her heart sank in a different way.

This wasn't going to be easy.

Chapter Thirteen

IF ONLY TRUST WAS EASY

THE EVENING PASSED WHILE Sheila managed—with great effort—to keep her questions to herself. She had told the Lord she would trust Him. Right now, she felt it went against every shred of common sense and natural human behavior for her not to ask Ryan anything, but she kept her mouth shut. *He's in Your hands, Lord*, she reminded Him.

Maybe she was reminding herself.

She and Ryan sat on the sofa together after tucking the kids in bed. She must have been looking at him strangely as she pondered the incident, because he caught her gaze and raised his brows.

"Did you want to say something?"

Her insides shouted, *YES! I sure do!* But it seemed like God Himself was stopping her. *Not yet,* the Holy Spirit seemed to whisper. She rose to gather a stack of DVDs on the floor that the kids had rifled through earlier. Amazing how much direction the Lord seemed to be giving her about this! She wished she could always feel so sure of His will.

How could she not obey?

She said, "Did *you* want to say something?" Maybe he'd open up of his own volition. Perhaps this was his chance to come clean without her prying.

"Yes," he said, nodding and gazing at her. "You're beautiful, my sweet wife."

Sheila smiled despite her disappointment. It was hardly the disclosure she hoped for. He rose and came to her, offering a hand to help her up. When she came to her feet, he spun her around so he could put his arms about her waist from behind. He kissed her neck.

"Thanks for being patient," he whispered.

Sheila swallowed but said nothing. She was only patient because the Lord was helping her be. Or should she say, *requiring* it? As Ryan spun her back around and leaned in to kiss her, landing his lips softly on hers and tightening his hold about her, she was glad that she'd listened.

For months, he'd seemed far away, even when he was home. For months, she'd missed his affection. His better mood of late was crossing over to their marriage, and she was grateful for that.

Even though he still hadn't told her anything.

Ryan drew back. "I love you, Sheel." He kissed her face and drew her close again.

Shelia's heart filled like a thirsty gas tank at the station. She couldn't even reply. She hadn't realized how much she needed to hear those words. She needed them often these days.

He said softly in her ear, "How about we go take advantage of that license we got after our wedding, hmm?"

That night as she prayed, Sheila thanked the Lord for helping her be obedient. Her real need, it turned out, wasn't to have the old Ryan back—he was still there, underneath the hurt and insecurity that prevented him from sharing his work with her. Nor did she need her mother to believe in him. She hadn't done so before even when he was doing great, so what difference did it make?

What she really needed was to lean into this newfound trust in God. Trust that surpassed understanding. Trust that surrendered its rights. As his wife, she had every right to know what Ryan was up to. She would have to continue to surrender it to the Lord.

It struck her that in doing so, she was giving up the worry of it, too.

Now it was God's problem. Good! *You handle it, Lord!*

Clara was on a school break with extra time and came to watch the kids the following day—four days before Christmas. Sheila hated to ask her, but Tessa had called to tell her to get down to the church common room. They had received a windfall of special items like small Christmas stollens, frozen chunked sweet potato and sausage casserole, sausage links, and cranberry relish, but they were going fast.

Sheila was grateful to have Clara. She could have brought the kids to the church, but it would be faster and easier without them, and she could stop and chat with Tessa.

The secretary was no happier about Gabe than before; nothing had changed, (as Sheila knew from Emma) and she was still sorry about having to quit the job. She had tried to tell Gabe about her feelings for him but couldn't.

Sheila listened compassionately, nodding at appropriate intervals. "Does he know you're leaving?" she asked.

Tessa nodded, her lips pursed. "I told him."

"How did he react?"

Her eyes wandered as she remembered. "He was sorry. He seemed very sorry," she acknowledged. "But not in the way I want him to be." She turned to Sheila with eyes filled with pain. "So when he and Emma get engaged, I'll go. It's the only way," she said, shaking her head, "for me to have a clear conscience before the Lord. If I stay, I'll always keep wanting Gabe for myself."

Sheila clucked her tongue. Gabe sure was obtuse! How could he miss the secretary's moony eyes and dogged devotion? How could he miss that Emma displayed neither of those things for him?

"I'm really hoping that won't happen. Their engagement still isn't set in stone."

Tessa looked up with a wisp of hope in her gaze. "Has Emma said yet if she'll accept him?"

Sheila considered how to answer without revealing anything Emma wouldn't want her to. Should she say that even if Emma accepted the ring, she would break up with Gabe later? And that she didn't want to break his heart on Christmas Eve, but she would have the strength to do it afterward?

"Let me put it this way," she said carefully. "I think you have good reason to hope. Just hang in there." She gave Tessa a heartfelt look. "We don't want to lose you! And Gabe doesn't, either."

Smiling sadly, Tessa said, "Thank you." Her eyes opened wider. "How are things between you and Ryan?"

Sheila told her that they were doing better as a couple, even though he still hadn't come forward about his activities. She told how she'd given it to the Lord, and how it seemed He was calling her to trust Him despite everything and just hold on and wait. "I'm *trying* to hang on to that," she admitted. "Ryan's secrecy could still drive me bananas if I let it. It just isn't right!"

Tessa agreed, "It isn't. But did you notice? We're both hanging on and waiting because of the man in our life!"

"It's true!" Sheila said, leaning her head forward.

Tessa continued, "Only sometimes I'm not doing it very well. When I pray, I feel like I'm just worrying out loud to God. It takes effort to stay in peace and trust."

"It does!" agreed Sheila. "But I have to admit, when I leave it with Him and don't nag Ryan about what he's doing or what his plan is, we get along so much better."

Tessa nodded understandingly. "Let's keep each other in prayer."

"Absolutely," said Sheila.

Tessa looked at her watch. "You better get to the common room. I don't want your family to miss the good stuff." She smiled encouragingly.

Suddenly Sheila's gaze was drawn to one side of the office where she saw rows of large, festively wrapped baskets in neat lines along the floor. Each was topped with a giant bow and looked so inviting and full of good things. She wondered who the lucky recipients were.

"Who all are they going to?" She went for a closer look, but Tessa had come around and sort of blocked her way.

"Only families who are *very* needy this year."

Sheila nodded, but a shaft of disappointment went through her. She felt her family was needy. However, they had food and clothes and shelter. Didn't Jesus say to be content with such things? There were people in much worse circumstances, such as those dealing with mortal illnesses, or those who recently lost a loved one.

"Yeah. I'll bet there are a lot of families who are worse off than we are." She took one last look. It would have been such a treat for the kids. Determined to conquer envy, she said, "I'm glad the church is doing something for them."

Chapter Fourteen

A Surprising Delivery

When Sheila got home, Clara and the kids were at the dining room table where she was demonstrating how to make an origami angel. They didn't come to greet her at the door or run after her into the kitchen to see what she'd brought home, so she knew they must be fascinated.

Jase was watching intently, head in both hands, while Kace was attempting to copy what Clara was doing.

"Hi, guys!" she smiled in at them.

"Hi, Mom!" Jase snapped to attention and ran toward her.

"Want to help me put this stuff away?"

He hugged her legs and planted a kiss on the region of her knee. "No. I'm watching Clara."

She shared a smile with the sitter. After hanging up her winter gear, she took her things to the kitchen.

As Clara prepared to leave, she asked if Sheila would be at the Christmas Eve potluck. The church held one annually, sometimes at the church, sometimes in homes of members. This year, it would be at Gabe's house.

Sheila said, "We're planning on it, but hold on a sec." She was afraid she'd forget it later, so she ran to the tree and got the little wrapped box with the "Thankful for you" heart bracelet she'd picked up in town.

Clara stared at the gift as though stunned, and a slow smile spread to her eyes. With earnestness she said, "Are you sure? You didn't have to get me anything!"

"You deserve more," Sheila said. "It's the least we could do."

Clara hadn't expected anything and yet was so willing a servant, babysitting for nothing in return. God's people did things like that, praise God.

"Thank you so much!" she said with shining eyes, as if Sheila had given her a crown jewel. She gave the sitter an impulsive hug. "The kids love you and we're so grateful for you."

After she left, Sheila was filling the kettle for a cup of tea when there was a knock at the door accompanied by the jingling Christmas bells.

Veering from the teapot, she went to answer it, wondering if it would be carolers. She gasped with delight when it opened to reveal Tessa holding one of the big, wrapped gift baskets! She exclaimed, smiling, "You're kidding! Oh, my gosh!"

She opened the door wider to usher her in, letting in a blast of cold air that whooshed in as well. Gabe was next, with a large, frozen turkey in one gloved hand and a bulging Christmas stocking in another. They stood there in the foyer smiling, bundled up in winter gear like Christmas elves.

"You two ought to be wearing Santa hats," Sheila said. "I can't believe this!"

Tessa glowed with satisfaction. "I feel like Santa today," she said, smiling.

She looked so pretty when she smiled.

She continued, "But this is from the church, as you know. We're only the messengers."

Surveying the basket and other goodies, Sheila's heart felt full. "This means so much. The kids will love this. Ryan will be grateful, too." She directed them where to put the things.

Still smiling widely, Tessa told her how difficult it was not to spill the beans earlier.

"You did a great job keeping it from me!" Sheila cried. "I had no clue." She glanced at Gabe who wore a little grin but his eyes were all for Tessa, admiring, gentle, as if he enjoyed seeing Tessa's delight at spreading cheer more than Sheila's delight in receiving it. She hoped Tessa noticed.

She gave them both a hug. "Thank you so much!" As they turned to go, she said, "Wait. Can you stay for a cup of tea or cocoa?"

"We still have more stops to make, but thank you," Tessa said. "And I almost forgot. The stocking is extra, from Emma and Ethan."

"Wow," Sheila said. She was blessed with such good friends. She must be sure to thank Emma later. She wondered if Gabe noticed the 'Emma and Ethan' part of that.

She wondered if Tessa noticed too.

She thanked them again, and Gabe left the house first. Before Tessa followed, Sheila gave her a knowing grin, nodding toward him outside. Tessa smiled sheepishly and steepled her hands into a praying pose.

Sheila whispered, "Yes! I'm praying."

As the door closed behind her, the kids came bounding up the stairs from where Clara had sent them earlier to clean up their toys and mess.

Kacie and Jase were fascinated by the basket and the stocking, asking questions, wanting to open it all, hovering around and touching what they could.

Sheila wouldn't let them open anything. "We'll wait until your father gets home," she said, quenching their excitement.

She placed the basket beneath the tree and hung the bulging stocking on a hook on the mantel. She didn't normally put out stockings until Christmas Eve after the kids were in bed. It made Christmas morning all the more special, she felt, to see them for the first time filled with small toys and trinkets.

She hoped Ryan would read the Christmas story as usual. They hadn't discussed it yet. He had begun reading the miraculous account from the Book of Luke while Sheila served a big breakfast, though only she and Ryan would eat it. The kids were usually too excited to play with their new things to eat.

Looking over the huge basket with its tantalizing goodies, Sheila reflected that while Grace Church wasn't large, its members were large-hearted. How blessed she was that Aspen Creek had a pulpit that spoke gospel truth while also encouraging the members to care for one another in ways such as this. They didn't forget the town, either. Anyone in need could come to the food pantry.

She remembered her disappointment earlier. She had thought her family didn't make the cut for basket recipients, yet God knew all along that they had.

Thank You, Lord!

Chapter Fifteen

DISCOVERY IN THE BANK ACCOUNT

SHEILA HAD ONLY GONE back for that cup of tea when Mrs. Henderson called. She was getting   last minute gifts in town and wished to stop by afterward. Sheila hoped she'd watch the kids long enough so she could disappear for awhile and call Emma. She *really* wanted to tell her about seeing Ryan the day before but hadn't had a chance.

There was no way she'd tell her mother.

"What stores are you going to?" she asked her.

"Just one. Amy's Amish Quilts for the all-natural hand cream and other skincare products they carry. They're great stocking stuffers."

"I was just there yesterday!" Sheila exclaimed. She told her mother about the kindness of Amy and Sunshine. "Too bad I didn't know you needed that stuff, I could have picked it up for you," she added while filling the kettle from the sink.

"How would you do that? With a credit card?" Her mother's tone implied that if Sheila used credit, it must be because they were flat broke.

She didn't reply.

"Anyway, most of it's for you, so you shouldn't be the one to get it."

Her mother was a stern woman in some ways, but she was generous. Sheila would use those skincare gifts all year.

"I'll come by afterward, if that's alright."

Surprised, Sheila said, "Sure. I'll have a pot of tea ready." She didn't usually come by so often. As she took out her favorite blue-and-white teapot, and two bags of Apricot tea, she hoped her mother's visit was not to nag her again about accepting a loan.

That reminded her—she'd better check their accounts. She might be able to say they were still okay and didn't need a loan—though she doubted it.

She grabbed her laptop and sat at the dining room table with the kids while they colored drawings for both sets of grandparents.

Ryan's parents weren't involved with their family other than Christmas and birthday cards for the kids. They hadn't been involved enough with Ryan when he was growing up. But Sheila told the kids to include them if they were making something for her parents, and they seemed eager to. They hoped to get their attention, she supposed. *Good luck with that.*

As she opened the laptop, her heart thudded. How many months had it been since she'd logged on to their accounts? Ryan did the lion's share of banking and bill paying. Now and then they'd discuss their savings, whether to make a purchase, invest more, donate more, or take more deductions from his paycheck for tax purposes. That sort of thing.

When he first got fired, he said they'd be okay. They had savings. He probably told her the figures at the time. Since then, he'd said numerous times they were still okay.

But she hadn't wanted to see for herself.

If she didn't know how bad off they were, she couldn't hold it against him.

Taking a deep breath, she told herself it was best that she knew the worst. Only a week ago it might have given her something concrete to present to Ryan so she could *demand* he tell her what he was doing before they couldn't pay their mortgage any longer.

But now she had forfeited her right to make demands. At least temporarily. *Trust meant believing without seeing. Trust meant not needing to know.*

In *this* case, based on how she believed the Lord wanted her to behave.

It wasn't a tactic she would recommend at large.

Even now, it only made sense *not* to pry because she could trust the Lord to do it for her. She wasn't being naïve or putting her head in the sand. She was actively trusting God. Was there a chance she could have got the message wrong? That it wasn't the Lord speaking to her but her own mind?

Yes, she knew that. It all boiled down to faith. She believed the Lord had spoken. He would show her in time if she was wrong.

It didn't mean she couldn't know the state of their finances, though.

And, if she were to see that things were indeed dire and she pointed it out, Ryan would have a chance to volunteer information to reassure her. What he was doing, what his plan was. He'd said all along that he would. There were only four more days until Christmas!

Her chest felt tight as she clicked on their savings account. Relief opened her lungs and she took a deep breath. The account was greatly reduced but she expected that. With what was left, she figured they could continue living off it for four or five more months. They weren't at the brink of bankruptcy.

Which meant she had no good reason to complain to Ryan about that.

She clicked on checking out of curiosity. To her shock, there was a four-day-old deposit of $5,000! A deposit, not a withdrawal—she checked twice to be sure.

Had Ryan found a new job without telling her? Was this a paycheck? How could he not mention this, knowing she'd be glad and relieved about it?

Excitement filled her. Maybe things were starting to turn around. For Ryan and the family! She clicked on the check to see who it was from.

Puzzlement, then disappointment, replaced excitement. It was a bank check. Anonymous.

Ryan hadn't mentioned it and the source of the money was a mystery. He evidently didn't want her to know about it. Just like he didn't want to include her in his daily business. She logged out with a heavy heart and shut the laptop.

Weariness came across her. The water was boiling. She poured it to fill the teapot, then let it steep, but she was moving slowly, as if sapped for strength.

What kind of company would pay its employees with generic bank checks? Was he doing something illegal? The image of him and Leon entering that old building resurfaced.

"Mommy, I'm telling Grandma and Grandpa about our paper angels and what we drew downstairs. Is shepherd p-e-r-d or p-h-e-r-d?"

"It's p-h-e-r-d," Sheila said. Didn't this mean she had no choice but to confront Ryan? Anyone in her position would want to know who that check was from.

It would mean an awful fight. She'd been trying not to rock the boat—to trust, as the Lord wanted her to. But wasn't this too much? How long was she supposed to turn a blind eye to things? How could she not be suspicious, under these circumstances? First, the old building, and now this.

The Christmas bells at the front door jingled and Mrs. Henderson let herself in. To Sheila's delight, her father came in right behind her.

"Dad! Hi!" She hurried to give him a hug. In seconds, the kids were all over him and he was barely able to get his coat off and into his wife's arms or greet Sheila before being dragged down the basement stairs by one arm to admire their handiwork from the other day.

Her mother hung the coats in the hall closet and then turned to her. "He didn't want me to tell you he was coming."

Sheila smiled. "That's Dad. We're just glad he's here!" She was doubly glad. It was a welcome distraction.

Mrs. Henderson's gaze wandered to the large, festive basket. "Is this from your church?"

Sheila nodded. "Yes! I saw a bunch of baskets in the secretary's office earlier but didn't think we'd be getting one!"

Her mother nodded approvingly but said, "Why on earth not? You certainly need it." She reached for the huge turkey. "I suppose you'll want this in the refrigerator to defrost?"

Sheila had intended to leave it out for an hour or two to start defrosting, since turkeys needed about four days in the refrigerator for that. She'd dealt with frozen gizzards before and it was no fun, to say the least.

She'd picked up a ham for Christmas, but she could use it on New Year's Eve. The turkey leftovers would go a long way until then. She'd make a hearty soup, and a casserole or two.

The day after Christmas, they were to eat at her parents' house. She prayed that Ryan would have good news before then or there would be tension coming from her mom, she was sure.

Following her mother into the kitchen, Sheila said, "Did you get what you wanted from Amy's?"

Mrs. Henderson nodded, "And more," she said, with her lips turned up. "So many nice Christmas things, they have!"

"They do. I love that store." Laughter floated up from downstairs. The kids loved playing with Grandpa. "Thanks for bringing Dad," she said as she poured herself and her mother a cup of steaming tea.

"He's happy to see the kids. But we also wanted to talk to you about taking that loan."

Sheila's stomach tightened. Impulsively, she blurted, "There's no need for that. Ryan earned $5,000 this week."

The older woman's eyes widened, her brows high. "Is that so? It's about time! What's he doing? He found a job?"

Sorry she'd said anything, Sheila turned toward the dining room. "Let's go sit and have our tea, but I don't want to talk about it."

Her mother tut-tutted with her tongue. "Not so fast, young lady."

"I'm not your young lady anymore, Mother," Sheila said firmly. "I'm a grown woman and a mother myself."

Mrs. Henderson's lips twitched. "I know that... How did he earn that money?"

She could see her mother was not going to let this drop. "I'm not sure." She hated having to say that, but it was true. "I only saw the check."

With widened eyes, her mother asked, "Who was it from?"

"It was a bank deposit check. It didn't say."

The older lady frowned. "And didn't you ask him about it?"

"I just saw it, literally minutes ago. I haven't had a chance yet."

The others came trudging back upstairs. Jase yawned, but he came and tugged on Sheila's hand. "Mommy, you said we'd look at Christmas lights today!"

"Tomorrow, honey. After dinner." To her mother she said, "I'll ask him."

Her father came and looked from his wife to Sheila, sensing the tension.

Mrs. Henderson shook her head, meeting his eyes. To Sheila she said, "He'd better give you a straight answer. No more of that 'I'll tell you soon' nonsense." She made a huffing sound. "He should have told you yesterday. He should have told you from the start."

She agreed with her mother's sentiments but didn't want to hear about it from her. "Mom, not in front of the kids, please. Let's have our tea." She hoped that would end the conversation. She turned to her dad. "Tea, Dad? Or hot cocoa?" He was heading for the living room but looked back and smiled mischievously. "I'll take the cocoa. If your mother lets me."

Sheila leaned in. "We won't ask her," she said in a loud whisper.

Thankfully, her mother only pursed her lips. When she added, "I'll put up the water," Sheila knew her news about Ryan earning money must have put her in a good mood.

And there was no more talk about a loan.

Her parents sipped their drinks in the living room with the kids while she readied things for dinner. The matter of the check was foremost in her mind. It was as if the proverbial demon on her shoulder was whispering in her ear. Wasn't the only plausible reason that he hadn't mentioned it in four days was because it wasn't earned honestly? That it might be from an illicit activity?

Maybe there's a perfectly good explanation.

It felt hard to believe that.

Just like her to give her worries to the Lord and then take them right back.

Chapter Sixteen

TRUSTING AND TALKING

WHEN SHEILA INVITED HER parents to stay for dinner, her dad said, "Sure! What're we having?"

Her mother said in a reproving tone, "Bill. I already put something aside for us tonight." She turned to Sheila with a meaningful look. "And I think this family needs more time to be by themselves." Sheila understood she meant to give her time to ask Ryan about the check.

She hardly needed the nudge. The worrisome matter of the anonymous check and what it meant hovered around her heart like a cloud of gnats, giving her no peace.

Pastor Mark's admonition came back to her. *Do you want peace? Give it to Jesus. Trust Him to handle it.* She hadn't known about the abandoned building or the check then. Would he say something differently if he knew?

There was such a thing as church discipline. Didn't Ryan's behavior warrant correction from his spiritual leaders? Why couldn't Mark have a good talk with Ryan and point out the sin of keeping such important matters from his wife?

She made a mental note to call him the following day. He was no doubt as busy as the next person this close to Christmas, but Sheila felt constrained to do *something* in light of these new developments.

Last week's question from the Lord came to mind: *What about Me? Can you trust Me to handle this? To handle Ryan?*

Lord, she prayed silently, *I can't tell if you've let me learn about the building and the check to nudge me to ask Ryan about them; or if You're still telling me to wait and trust. What should I do?*

The only "answer" she got, if it was an answer, was that the verse "Jesus Christ, the same yesterday, today, and forever," from the book of Hebrews, came to mind.

She sighed. Jesus Christ, the same...

And suddenly she realized there was a great blessing in that verse. *Thank You for not changing. You are always faithful. You always keep your promises. You always have our good in mind.*

Giving thanks seemed to clear the air for her. He was faithful. No matter what. This didn't mean she had to be a martyr. Or a door mat. Or a silent sufferer forever.

It didn't depend on HER.

And that was a great relief. Ryan wouldn't like it, but it was time for her to get answers.

Her mother would grill her about where the money had come from, and it would look like she was afraid of him if she didn't ask. That *would* be burying her head in the sand.

When Ryan came home for dinner, the kids hopped around him, telling him of their fun day, first with Clara, and then their grandparents. When they settled down, Sheila told him she wanted to talk to him later.

He nodded slowly, studying her expression.

Kacie said, "Is something not okay, Mommy? What do you need to talk to Daddy about?"

"Everything's fine, sweetheart," Ryan said smoothly, pre-empting any response by Sheila. "We'll talk about Christmas! How's that for okay?"

Kace grinned. "That's very okay!"

"Yeah!" piped in Jase.

"Talk about our presents!" Kace smiled happily at her brother.

"Yeah, our presents!" he echoed.

After dinner, the kids begged them to join them for one of their favorite Christmas movies. To her relief, Ryan agreed. She often felt edgy after dinner, waiting to see if it would be an office night, in which case he'd disappear for the evening, or, like tonight, if he'd stay with the family.

When he looked her way after agreeing to watch, she gave him an approving nod.

During the movie, she planned what would be best to say to him later. In her mind, no matter how she framed the conversation, they would end up fighting.

If her parents hadn't stayed so long, she would have called Emma to get her thoughts on the matter. Talking to her friend helped her sort through befuddling things. But she hadn't had the chance.

Silently, she prayed. *Lord, I am trusting this situation to You. I'm trusting You to give us a good, truthful conversation...*

The movie continued, though she wasn't taking it in.

An enlightening one...

The others laughed at the screen, but she hardly noticed.

Give us a breakthrough, my God. Help us to draw closer to each other! Help Ryan to open up to me! We need this!

Ryan rose and stirred the fire in the grate. She liked that he'd been burning logs every night even when he disappeared upstairs afterward. Combined with their glowing Christmas tree, soft white lights along the wide windowsill in the room, and "Merry Christmas" pillows on the sofa and loveseat, the fire gave a warm, happy holiday feeling.

But heaviness was still there. She kept praying. *I'm going to talk to him in faith, trusting that You're in charge of this conversation. Trusting that You will cause it to work for good in our lives.*

After the movie, getting into PJs and brushing teeth, Sheila read the kids their nightly Advent devotional. Ryan joined them for their bedtime prayer and together they tucked them in. Any time now, Sheila thought, they'd need to move Jase out of Kace's room. He had one half of it, and his own bed, and she was only seven. But growing up so fast. She'd want her privacy.

Ryan touched her arm and motioned for them to go back downstairs. Their talk. Anticipation, fear, anxiety. All ran through her. *Wait. Trust, trust.*

And then she realized Ryan wasn't angry that she wanted it. That was a change. That was a *good* change. *Thank You, Lord.*

Chapter Seventeen

MISTLETOE

SHEILA SUGGESTED THEY SIT in the living room. They used to sit at the kitchen table over a cup of tea and a snack for late talks. Tonight, she only wanted to talk.

As they reached the bottom of the stairs, Kacie came scampering down after them.

"What's up, Kace?" Sheila asked.

Ryan said, "Why are you out of bed?"

She shot past them both and ran to the sofa, then held up Trixie, a girl teddy bear with a chiffon pink skirt and a faux pearl necklace. Trixie was a favorite since Kace's fourth birthday when she got her. She was very careful to keep her clean. The doll still looked pretty good considering all the many places it had traveled with her, car trips, vacations, runs to the store, and so on. At bedtime, it sat at the end of Kace's bed where she could see it in the soft glow of her nightlight.

"I forgot my bear," she said, heading back toward them. She stopped suddenly and pointed up at a sprig of greenery hanging from the doorframe to the room. "Mommy hung mistletoe, Daddy. You should take her there and kiss her!"

Ryan looked dazed. To Sheila he said, "What are they teaching kids these days?"

Sheila's lips twitched. She'd forgotten all about the mistletoe. It wasn't the most realistic, being only .99 at Snowberry's; she'd hung it purely as a decoration, not even thinking about kissing.

He said to Kace, "Go to bed. I'll handle kissing Mommy."

"I want to see it!" she cried.

Ryan glanced at Sheila who was trying to repress her grin. She was determined to remain neutral. She had a serious conversation ahead with this man and wasn't exactly in a kissing mood.

He took her hand and led her to stand underneath the mistletoe, and then put his arms about her, drawing her close. "Don't mind if I do," he said in a low tone with a little smile. Sheila couldn't help but enjoy, as she always did, his manliness, his broad shoulders and strength. His eyes were locked on hers, and then he leaned down and kissed her.

His mouth felt warm, his embrace, secure. He ended the kiss, pulled away and looked at Kacie as if to say, "There."

She giggled. "That wasn't a real kiss, Daddy! The Prince kissed Cinderella better than that."

"Oh, did he!" Ryan chuckled, his arms still around Sheila.

Kacie nodded, smiling. She looked like a little Christmas angel in her white, frilly nightgown and a halo of dark locks. An angel bringing them together.

"Go to bed!" Ryan cried, but his lips were turned up at the sides.

Kace frowned, turned and walked up two steps, and there she stopped. Turning around again she said firmly and with her little face puckered seriously, "I'll go to bed after you give Mommy a *real* kiss!"

Ryan's brows rose. "You'll go to bed when I tell you to, you little rascal."

She waited, lifting her chin impishly at him like a boss who'd just issued an order.

Ryan hadn't let go of Sheila. He studied her eyes and moved aside a stray tress of hair from her face. Without looking away, he called to Kace. "You ready?"

"Ready and wait-ting," she replied in a sing-song voice as if he was taking too long.

With a chuckle, he drew Sheila closer. He kissed her cheek and then drew back enough to lower his lips onto hers.

And gave her a real kiss. Sheila felt like she was getting a long, cool drink on a hot day.

She almost broke it up after about ten seconds. It seemed like a long time to kiss in front of one's eight-year-old. Even though she loved every second. Entwined with Ryan like that, it was as if the past year hadn't happened, as if he'd never changed. As if all was well.

She felt loved. Just like the week before when he'd been so affectionate.

When his kiss deepened, she knew he was enjoying their closeness, that he wanted more of it too. But she pressed gently against him. He took the cue and closed the kiss.

Without releasing her, he turned his head to Kacie on the stairs.

"That was a real kiss, Daddy! You did it!"

"Go to bed!" he said again, trying to sound severe and not laugh.

Sheila called, "Goodnight, sweetie," with a smile on her face. That girl!

She went to move from his arms, but he said, "Whoa. What's your hurry?" And he kissed her again. A few minutes later, he took her hand and looked toward the stairs.

"I know you wanted to talk, but...maybe later?"

She nodded. Her husband could always make her heart flutter, and it was fluttering now. He still hadn't revealed his secrets—with Christmas so close, he was running out of time. But suddenly it felt less important.

He led them up the steps but stopped every few feet and drew her close and kissed her face, her nose, her mouth; he did that all the way to their bedroom.

"I love you, Sheel. I need you." His voice sounded ragged, but oh, so sweet.

"I love and need you too!"

She still didn't know what her husband was doing to earn that money. Nor did she know what was going on inside that abandoned building.

But now was not the time to confront him. He was with her, he loved her, he was happy. This is what mattered. It was enough.

For now.

Chapter Eighteen

ENOUGH IS ENOUGH (WHAT BRIELLE SAID)

SHEILA CALLED EMMA THE following morning. Her friend was suffering more than ever, torn between following her heart or her head. Her heart said, break up with Gabe because you're in love with Ethan. But her head said, you can't break Gabe's heart now! Not at Christmas! Think of the poor guy's past. Dumped on Christmas Eve five years ago.

Sheila encouraged her to follow her heart. "You're not doing Gabe any favors by holding onto him. He's not the one you want. He deserves someone who loves him." She thought of poor Tessa, who really loved Gabe. She wished she could tell Emma, but Tessa had asked her not to. She knew Emma had pretty much figured it out anyway.

"I do love Gabe," Emma replied weakly.

"Like a brother in the Lord. You love Ethan like a man you want to marry. You and he are a lot alike, and you understand each other."

Emma sighed. "I know." After a pause she said, "How are you doing? Has Ryan told you yet?"

Ah, yes, the reason she called Emma to begin with. Her thoughts exploded. She felt closer to Ryan than she had in months. They were sharing time together as man and wife more regularly. But all the new developments of what she knew came rushing out. She told about the check, and how she'd seen Ryan and Leon disappear into that old building. She told her how she felt the Lord was telling her to trust Him despite all of that, and how very difficult that was.

"Wait. That old building next door to Maple & Main? That's where the construction is going on! They're working for that construction company! Remember, we heard the noise when we were there?"

"Oh my word, OF COURSE!" That was it. She was an idiot. Reeling with the revelation, she realized Ryan had been working right beneath her nose! Why was she so obtuse? Because she was too quick to think the worst, not the best. She hadn't succeeded in giving Ryan the benefit of the doubt at all.

"Emma, I am so, so, stupid! How could I not realize that?"

"Because you're too close to it," she said kindly. "You've got the kids and Christmas and shopping and cooking and baking and then Ryan being weird and secretive... it's understandable."

She was so thankful for Emma's friendship. "Thank you. But you're just being nice. I really am stupid."

"Stop it!" her friend scolded. "You've had a very tough year. Go easy on yourself."

"I saw him and Leon talking at church, and Brielle said Leon wanted to be a partner in a new startup. Wait... do you think the construction firm is Ryan? Ryan and Leon, starting their own business?"

"I don't know," Emma said. "But it sounds like it."

"I'm going to call Brielle and see what she thinks."

"Let me know."

"And let me know when you get brave and tell Gabe you love his brother."

"Sheel! My plan is to wait until after the holiday. It'll be less hard on him."

"But what about his proposal? Are you going to accept?"

There was a pause. A sigh. "I don't know! I should, but I don't know."

"You shouldn't." She paused. "And by the way, the kids are so excited about that stocking. Thank you so much. You're such a good friend."

"Ethan helped a lot with that. He is crazy generous."

A minute later she went to call Brielle, but her phone buzzed. "Brielle! I was just going to call you."

"Really?" Her strong, smooth voice always surprised Sheila. Brielle was tall but had a delicate looking kind of beauty. Her voice conveyed confidence.

"I wanted to let you know that Leon no longer needs my money. He said the other guy can put out $25,000 and that in lieu of the money, Leon will agree not to take any payment until his share is covered by profits."

"Oh." Sheila and Emma's idea that the two men were in on the same business dissipated like an oasis just when she thought she'd reached it.

"Is that a bad thing?" Brielle asked.

Sheila told her how she'd seen the men together in town, about the new addition to Maple & Main, and how it had looked like they might be the new construction company behind the work.

"I think they are," Brielle said. "Considering what you saw. Ryan might have been showing his 'partner' the progress of that addition."

"But Ryan doesn't have $25,000. If he had that money, I think I'd know."

"Hmmm." There was a silence. "What about a 401K? He worked long enough to build one, didn't he?"

Sheila thought about it. "Well, now that you mention it, his company grew like crazy while Ryan was there, and I think they did dump a huge bonus each year in all the managers' 401K accounts. I didn't consider it spending money for us, so I forgot all about it! Do you really think he could have built up that much in only a few years? He mentioned it to me in the past, but I'm not a numbers person."

That was putting it lightly. She could never remember amounts. Except for that check. Five thousand dollars was emblazoned on her brain.

"If his company did really well, and he got special perks, he definitely could have. I've known of managers getting 40% bonuses on top of their salaries. And he must be getting the money from somewhere," she pointed out.

"Assuming he is the business partner," Sheila said.

"Right." Brielle paused. "You know what? I'm sick of this. I'm telling Leon to spill it, or I'll break our engagement. It's ridiculous, this mysteriousness!"

"You know what?" Sheila replied. "I'm sick of it too. In fact, I've had it! I'm going to talk with Ryan tonight."

"I'll talk with Leon. I'll call you tomorrow," she said.

Sheila felt so restless and disturbed. She really didn't need this drama right before Christmas. Ryan was putting her through so much when it was unnecessary! If all he was doing was starting a business, that was a good thing! Why keep it a secret?

Kace had asked for ravioli for lunch, so she set a pot of water to boil. When bubbles began rising in it, she felt like it mirrored her insides, bubbling with possibilities. *Good ones*. What a change that was. Anticipation not shadowed by fear and doubt. Ryan was starting a business! In a field he loved. The only troubling thing was the secrecy he insisted on around it.

She could hardly wait for him to get home.

As the hours ticked past, she realized she and Brielle could be wrong. She'd have to be careful of what she would say. And how she would say it.

Just to be sure of her facts, she checked on the kids and then logged onto their bank account to review the date on that check. She would present him with the evidence, tell him what Leon had said, and how she'd seen him and Leon in town. It was now three days until Christmas, and he had promised to tell her anyway. Not to mention that she deserved to know.

When she clicked on the account, there was a fresh withdrawal of five thousand dollars. That money from the check was gone.

Brielle said Leon no longer needed five thousand from her.

That could not be a coincidence!

Chapter Nineteen

NOT THIS TIME

SHEILA DECIDED NOT TO call Pastor Mark until she tried speaking with Ryan. If even now, three days before Christmas, he still refused to be transparent with her, then she would call the pastor for advice and prayer.

The children seemed tired and were quietly sitting in the living room. Sheila wandered upstairs and went by Ryan's office. She stopped. She tried the door. It wasn't locked.

For some reason she had never tried to snoop around for clues for what he was doing.

Suddenly, she wanted to.

She opened the door and looked around. The office hadn't changed. The same bookshelves with home building books, construction, home improvement and plumbing. A few spy fiction titles. A few grid-down suspense titles. A shelf of theological books, Bibles, and Christian living themes. One jumped out at her. *Husbands, Love Your Wives.*

She almost pulled it off to leave in a conspicuous place. Ryan was more affectionate again and made her feel loved on the one hand, but his continued secrecy did the opposite. And she was sure that a Christian book on marriage would never condone such behavior.

She went near the desk and saw a folder on top of his laptop. Ah! This surely would be revealing!

She reached out to pick it up. Her hand hovered over the folder... and hovered.

She withdrew it. She turned and left the room, carefully shutting the door behind her.

Ryan had told her over and over that he needed her to trust him. If he found out she'd peeked at his stuff, he'd be hurt. Possibly furious.

It was wrong of him.

But it's where he was at for the time being.

The Lord had encouraged her to trust HIM. If she peeked, how was she obeying Him?

Her conscience would bother her if she looked, and that was the end of it.

She got dinner in the oven, easily done since her mother had left a meatloaf and mashed potatoes at her last visit. Sheila had only to reheat them and add a side of broccoli. The children would eat broccoli if she cooked it without garlic and added a liberal sprinkling of cheddar cheese, butter, and a few dashes of salt. She left it all in a warm oven and joined the kids in the living room. Together, they waited for Daddy to come home.

She browsed phone messages, and then the church app for new prayer requests. There were none.

The minutes ticked by.

Her phone buzzed. A text from Ryan. *Sorry, Sheel, but I'll be home late tonight. Gotta meet with someone.*

Hurt and disappointment washed over her. Was he going back to staying out late again? Her first impulse was to call him right then and there. To ask, who are you meeting with? He should have told her that.

She figured he wasn't going to, and her asking wouldn't help.

To prevent tears, she closed her eyes. *Wait. Stop.* She was thinking the worst. One late night didn't mean there would be more. She must give him the benefit of the doubt. It still didn't come naturally to do that.

Pray. She ought to pray. She needed help.

I give my hurt and disappointment to You, Lord. Keep me from jumping to wrong conclusions. Keep me from getting bitter about this. Maybe this meeting is about his business startup; it could be perfectly legitimate, even though he gave me no details. But please, cause him to come clean to me! I've been keeping silent in faith so You can act! Please, God, reveal what is hidden. Let us get past this chapter of our lives. Let us have a truly merry Christmas.

She swallowed the hurt and put on a smile for the kids.

"Daddy will be home late, guys, so let's go eat." She rose from the sofa.

"Why will Daddy be late, Mommy?" Kacie looked up at her. Jase looked up too.

Give him the benefit of the doubt. "I'm not sure, sweetheart. He must have something important to do." If Brielle was right and he was starting a business, she supposed keeping late hours was part and parcel of that.

"Like what?" Kacie's eyes were large and innocent, her question pure curiosity.

Sheila wondered the same thing. "He has a meeting," was the best answer she could give.

THAT EVENING SHE FELT weary and managed to get the kids and herself to bed earlier than usual. Why wait up for Ryan when he would be tight-lipped about his evening anyway?

Dark thoughts began converging in her brain like vultures discovering a corpse. Tears surfaced. She was weary from holding out. Weary of committing everything to God and seeing no change. Weary of Ryan's secrecy!

Maybe she should threaten again to go to her parents' house. Would that scare him enough to come to his senses and open up to her? Brielle was right. This secrecy was ridiculous! How long was she supposed to tolerate it?

Chapter Twenty

SHEILA'S CHRISTMAS BLESSING

"SHEEL, YOU AWAKE?"

She'd heard Ryan come in but had said nothing. She didn't know how late it was, she only knew she'd been trying to turn off the dark thoughts, to rest in faith and peace, but hadn't been very successful. Nor could she sleep.

Facing away from him, she sighed. "Yes."

"Can we talk?"

This sounded promising, though she expected it to be disappointing. Probably painful, too. She sat up and waited.

He came and sat down heavily beside her. He sighed. "I guess I've been *too* secretive."

She held back the sarcasm that flew to her thoughts. *Too secretive? Ya think?* "Yes?" was all she said.

Ryan's eyes were lowered, his face dark. Barely she could see that he had that sporty evening shadow of a beard around his jaw, but she hardened her heart. It didn't matter right now.

He clicked on the light.

Still not meeting her eyes, he said "I just felt ... defeated... when I thought about telling you what I'm up to when I didn't know for sure that it would succeed."

He looked up. His eyes were filled with pain, sorrow, regret.

Her heart warmed and ached for him at the same time. And felt annoyed. "Why would that make you feel defeated? Why couldn't it help to know I'm in it with you? That we're in it together?"

He looked even more hurt. She hated to see that in his eyes.

"Maybe it should have. But it didn't. I felt like, the more you know, the more you'd be waiting for me to fail at."

Ouch! That was so untrue!

Sheila thought before answering. *Help me, Lord! What do I say?* And suddenly she knew. "YOU are waiting for you to fail. I am waiting only for you to stop pushing me away!"

Ryan looked struck. His face crumpled and she thought for a moment that he might cry! He had never cried in front of her. She didn't know if he ever cried at all. But that look about broke her heart.

She hurriedly added, "I have no reason to think you'll fail at anything you put your heart into doing. I have faith in you! I have always had faith in you. You're brilliant at what you do, talented, a hard worker, a good father, a believer—you're everything I ever wanted! Getting fired didn't change that."

She threw herself into his arms and he crushed her to his chest, breathing hard.

"I love you, Sheel," he whispered. "I need you so much!" He kissed her hair and her forehead. His voice sounded ragged and again, it broke her up.

"I love you, and I need you too!" She kissed his cheek and forehead, nose and lips. When he kissed her, Sheila felt like she'd been welcomed home after being out in the cold. He drew her closer and continued the kiss and she wrapped her arms around him while his love wrapped and soothed her heart.

Her whole mind and body relaxed. Things were going right now, as if peace and hope and joy were re-emerging after a long winter's hibernation.

He gently drew back and stroked the side of her face. "I'm sorry for how hard I've made this for you. At first, I was waiting until I knew for sure that I could support us. I just couldn't stand the idea that you would know if I tried but failed."

"Why not? We all fail at things."

He nodded. "In my case it felt final. It felt dire. I needed to prove myself. I needed to know I could earn money consistently. I got one job, and I was encouraged, but I needed to land other contracts. And if I did, I thought that would be a great surprise, a Christmas blessing, and I wanted to keep it under wraps until then. I'm sorry."

He shook his head. "Proverbs says 'The Lord detests lying lips, but he delights in people who are trustworthy.' I convinced myself since I wasn't lying to you, that I was being honest. And I know I'm trustworthy—I just didn't know if I could succeed. I didn't want to give you proof that your mother's right about me."

Sheila gasped. "NOTHING would ever convince me of that! My mother's attitude is inexcusable." She paused. "And you should know that I will love you no matter what. Fail or succeed, I *love* you."

He squeezed her hand. "I'm sorry, Sheel. I didn't trust you to love me no matter what."

"You didn't!" she agreed, vehemently.

"This afternoon I spent time with the Lord. I saw this verse in Second Corinthians." He pulled a slip of paper from his shirt pocket and read: "We have renounced secret and shameful ways; we do not use deception, nor do we distort the word of God. On the contrary, by setting forth the truth plainly, we commend ourselves to everyone's conscience in the sight of God."

He looked up at her plaintively. "I haven't been engaging in 'shameful' ways or trying to use deception." He paused, searching her eyes. "But I did use secret ways; and I did not reveal the truth plainly, though you of all people deserve that."

He pressed his lips together. "Can you forgive me?" His eyes were deep pools of vulnerability, large and dark with uncertainty.

"Yes, of course!" He grasped her in a bear hug, but she pressed against him and he drew back to search her eyes.

"It would be a lot easier for me," she said, "if you would finally tell me everything!" She rose to her knees and started pummeling him with her pillow. "Who did you meet with tonight? What have you been doing? What was your surprise?"

Chuckling and trying to deflect the pillow, he said, "That's what I came to do, really! I'll tell you everything!"

She lowered the pillow. "Hold on. Let's go down and get cozy. Tea or cocoa?"

MINUTES LATER, RYAN STOKED the fire and added a log. Sheila brought in cups of hot tea and a tray with caramel popcorn in bowls. She sat beside him and said, "Okay. Talk."

He nodded. "I'm starting my own construction company—."

Sheila couldn't contain herself. "I thought so! Whoop, whoop!"

His brows rose. "You did? You guessed?"

"Well, Brielle guessed. Based on Leon's wanting to borrow money so he could be 'someone's' business partner. And then," she paused and gave him a dead serious look. "I saw you and Leon in town. You went into that old, abandoned building right next to—"

"Maple & Main," he said in unison with her.

She nodded. "And I was too stupid to realize you were working on that addition, so I worried a lot and had to give it to the Lord."

"I'm sorry," he squeezed her hand. "Yeah. I found that building and the owner walked me through, and God just filled my brain with ideas. I knew I had to have it and start there."

"How did you afford it?" she asked. She'd mention the check she discovered soon.

He smiled. "I didn't. Amber Branson bought it and hired me to renovate it."

Sheila gasped. "Wow! How did that happen?"

He said, "After I looked through it, I met with Amber." He gave her a sideways look. "That was the day I wore office clothes, if you noticed."

"Of course I noticed! I thought you'd found a job."

"Well, I did, in a way. I told her she was losing money by not expanding and I could make an addition to her business that could double her income. I gave her plenty of possibilities of how to utilize the space. She said she'd been wanting to expand for a long time! She negotiated a price with the owner, and I drew up some plans for her to approve. After I started the work, she wrote out the first check."

"For five thousand dollars," Sheila said.

He bit his lip. "I thought you might notice."

"But then it disappeared. Where did the money go?"

"Back into the business." He looked steadily at her. "I found office space for rent out on Highway 29 and set up shop there."

"You ought to be on Main Street!" she cried.

"Maybe one day."

Sheila said, "I should have known immediately that you were working on that addition. I was so worried and anxious, my mind was clouded, I guess."

They sipped their drinks.

"Why did you need to lock yourself into your study all those nights?"

"Drawing up blueprints and contracts. First for a business partner—

"Leon," she said.

He quirked his lip to one side. "Yeah. I guess that was obvious." He paused. "Then for Amber Branson." He swallowed. "I also had to register the business with the state, apply for an LLC, get the license to operate as well as insurance against liability. I had to write a business plan in case I needed to borrow money or raise capital."

He paused, and took a breath as of a satisfied man. "We're now insured, licensed and bonded," he said proudly.

He continued, "I needed permits from the county, and I invested in office software for accounting and project management."

She nodded, thinking. This was all wonderful news.

In a way.

"I feel sad that you did all this without me. I would have loved to be part of it. I'm sure there were things I could do. I could have been your secretary. I can do paperwork."

"You would want to do that?" he asked. "Really?"

"Yes, really! I was a front desk secretary for a law firm, remember." She paused. "And there's no way I'd ever let you hire a young pretty secretary unless it's me!"

He grinned. "There's no way I'd want to. We'll work it out with the kids and all."
His eyes surveyed her. "You'll have to learn the software."

"I can do that," she said confidently. She'd used certain programs for the law firm.
She'd invest whatever time it took.

His eyes sparkled at her. "That'll save us money right there, when I don't have to
hire someone."

"*Us*," she repeated softly. "That is a beautiful word to me."

He leaned over and planted a warm kiss on the side of her face. "Me, too."

Sheila put her tea down and snuggled against him. Instantly, a strong arm went
around her and gently rubbed her back.

"So that was your big surprise."

"There's more to it."

She popped her head up. "Like what?"

"*As we speak*, I am waiting for two contracts to come back . Right here in town."

He squeezed her arm.
"Contracts that will mean a lot of money for us." He paused and his voice softened.
"They'll mean my business is really *in* business. My plan was to wait to tell you until
I had them in the bag. Signed and sealed. For your sake, I told them I absolutely had
to have their signatures before Christmas or the deal would be off. And they agreed!
I'm just waiting for the email with the attachments."

"You've done so much." She looked at him admiringly. "I felt the Lord kept telling
me to wait and trust HIM to help you and us." She smirked. "I would have nagged at
you a lot more if He hadn't. I would have worried more than I did, too." She nodded,
thinking about it. "To be precise, He said to give you the benefit of the doubt."

Ryan's brows rose. "He did?" He nodded slowly. "Thank you. Thanks for telling
me that. I felt for a long time like He'd abandoned me. But I know that was never
true. If I had found a job, I would never have started my own business. If I hadn't
gotten fired, I wouldn't have!"

"God is good," she agreed.

"Amen. He takes what we see as failure and turns it for our good." He took one
of her hands and raised it to his lips for a warm kiss. "I feel like this is really what I'm
meant to do."

Taking a deep breath, he said "I'm sorry for all the angst you went through. If it helps, Amber's second check should be in our account today or tomorrow. A *much* bigger check than the first one."

She nodded. That was nice to know, but she couldn't erase her sadness that he'd left her out for so long. It made her feel forgotten and neglected, and those feelings went deep.

"There's still one more thing I haven't told you."

She looked at him expectantly. There was a sparkle in his eyes.

"The name of the company. Sheila Construction. That was my biggest surprise, but I didn't want to tell you in case it didn't get off the ground."

Sheila's jaw dropped. "You're kidding!"

He leaned down and kissed her cheek. "I'm not. Technically, it's Sheila Construction and Renovations, LLC. But I think of it as Sheila Construction. Honestly, Sheel, I had you and the kids in mind all along. I know you felt neglected, but I had this driving need to get the company on good footing and I had to do whatever it took."

She felt as if he'd read her mind.

"I did feel neglected. And unimportant."

He squeezed her hand again. "I hate that," he said, his gaze turning sorrowful. He shook his head. "It took longer than I hoped but when I think about it, the whole thing happened fast. But every step took time. Finding prospective clients and meeting with them. Drawing up blueprints to show them what we could do for them, researching contracts and hiring a business lawyer to get them written. Not to mention inspecting the properties they wanted work done for or to put new construction on. And then I had to hire help to get it done in time."

He nodded. "Even though I wasn't paying out of profits yet, it felt good to give a few men work before Christmas. They were good. I'll keep them on."

She nodded. "I guess I can say I'm glad you did all that, although I still wish you'd have let me in on it."

He nodded. "I know. I'm sorry. I wish I could do it over differently."

Her brows furrowed. "You never told me who you met with tonight."

"Oh!" He grinned. "Leon. He requested the meet up. He wanted to tell me he'd revealed everything to Brielle, and how she'd scolded him for his secrecy—for *our* secrecy. He said he had no choice because she threatened to break off their engagement."

Sheila said, "Is that why you came clean tonight? Because you knew Brielle would spill the beans if you didn't?" If that were so, their whole talk would be ruined.

He shook his head. "No! I told Leon exactly what I told you about those Bible verses and that I had decided to tell you everything tonight anyway." He stared ahead, remembering. "He couldn't believe the timing of it. We talked more about it and we agreed that we're both dorks for not telling you and her sooner, but me especially, since I made him promise not to."

He looked at her remorsefully. "I was an insecure idiot. I can't tell you how sorry I am."

She repressed a smirk. "Oh, yes you can. Tell me how sorry you are!"

He grinned, got his arm around her and pulled her onto his lap. His breath tickled her ear as he said, "I am wholly, earnestly, eternally, terribly, sorry. I was so wrong. I dishonored you and our marriage. I dishonored the Lord, and my witness for Him."

He planted a kiss on her mouth. "I hope that naming the company for you shows how crazy I am about you, and that the rewards of this business will be the biggest Christmas blessing for you since Jesus!"

She shook her head with a little smile. "It's funny. I thought I wanted that. To see you back to work, bringing home money, happy again. And I'm thrilled that you've achieved that. But what I wanted most of all was you." She pulled her head away to meet his eyes. "Just you. Your honesty, your trust, your heart. *You* are the biggest Christmas blessing I could get this year."

Chapter Twenty-One

TALES AND TEACUPS

THE BEST THING ABOUT the reconciliation with Ryan was the aftermath. Sheila told Emma she felt like they were on a second honeymoon.

The morning after the "big reveal" as she now thought of it was sweet. Unbeknownst to her, Ryan had contacted Clara. When she showed up at the front door, Sheila's eyes widened.

"Hi! C'mon in. Is something up?"

Clara smiled as she walked in. "Mr. Preston asked me to come. I can stay for as long as you need. I brought my knitting." She held up a knitting caddy from which a few stray loops of yarn dangled out. Opening it, she withdrew a wrapped present. "This goes under the tree for the kids."

Sheila felt a warm glow inside because Ryan had arranged for the sitter to come. He had a surprise in store! And for once, she didn't mind not knowing.

She took the present. "Thank you! Though that wasn't necessary." The kids would be pleased, though.

"I wanted to," Clara returned, setting her caddy down. She took off her snow-laden boots on the waterproof mat near the door. She removed her coat, hung it in the closet and then her hat and gloves. Clara was Mary Poppins neat and always made the kids clean up before she left. A true angel of a girl.

Sheila said, "At least we can pay you now!"

Clara blushed. "Mr. Preston told me that, thank you."

Sheila smiled. "You can call us Sheila and Ryan." They'd known Clara for years, but it seemed awkward now that she was a young adult in college to keep up the formalities.

Clara bit her lip. "I'll try. Thanks."

"The kids are in the kitchen," she said, motioning with her head toward the room. "Have you eaten?"

"I haven't, actually," she said, picking up the caddy to deposit it near the doorway to the living room.

Ryan came sailing down the stairs. "Clara, thank you for coming!" His strong voice reached the kitchen; the kids came tearing out.

"Are you going out?" Jase asked Sheila.

"Where are you going?" Kacie asked.

Ryan said, "We're just going to town, we won't be out all day and later we'll go for that drive to see the lights and displays."

"Yipee!" shouted Jase, with a jump into the air.

"Go finish your breakfasts," Sheila said, smiling.

Jase smacked a kiss on the region of her knees and Kacie said flatly, "See you later," as though she was accepting an unwelcome situation.

"Well, hi!" Clara said as she followed them into the kitchen. "I'm glad to see you too!"

"Sorry," Sheila heard Kace and then Jase echo. "We just don't want Mommy and Daddy to go out."

Ryan held Sheila's coat for her and then got his own. Her gloves were in her coat pockets. She said, "Do you want coffee before we go? I just put it up."

"Clara will have some. Let's not. I'm going to show you where I've been going and what I've been doing."

Her heart rose like air bubbles in water. "I can't wait!"

"We'll eat at your favorite café while we're at it, since it now has a brand-new addition." In a playful tone he added, "An addition that isn't shoddy by half, if I say so myself." He held the door of the car open for her and ushered her in with one hand across her back.

"Is the café open today?" Some stores were closed in town for the whole week leading up to Christmas while others stayed open for last minutes sales as long as they could.

He nodded. "Mmm-hmm. I asked Amber yesterday."

He got in the car and the garage door opened with a button. He backed out and they set off.

"Thank you for doing this," Sheila said. "For calling Clara. I don't mind this kind of surprise."

"I owe you, Sheel," he said, moving his gaze from the road to glance at her.

She pondered whether to refute that. But didn't. After all, she felt like he did owe her for putting her through so much uncertainty and grief.

They fell quiet. Then, turning to her he said, "Don't expect anything *too* great."

Ryan did excellent work, but this was hard for him anyway, she realized. He always felt ready to fail the scrutiny of his closest family.

Hoping to erase the boyish trepidation, his sudden insecurity, that she was sure was completely unfounded, she said, "I'm sure it's beautiful! But even if it isn't, I care most that we're on the same page now. You're not locked away from me anymore."

He nodded and kissed the air toward her.

On an impulse, she added, "Honey, I will love you for the rest of our days, no matter what happens. You don't have to worry about failing at anything. It would never change my love for you."

He let out a breath and shook his head and gave her a look full of appreciation. "I don't deserve you."

"But you believe me, right? You know I'll always love you?"

He turned onto Main Street, but Sheila ignored the sights that usually filled her with warmth. She was focused only on Ryan.

"I guess I know that. Or maybe I don't know it the way I need to. I don't know it about God's love the way I need to, either."

She said lovingly, "We both love you and we both always will!"

He nodded. "Saved by faith through grace. Not by works. Not by anything I can do—or anything I fail at doing."

"Exactly."

"Thanks, Sheel."

Alicia came bustling toward them as soon as they entered the café, her face filled with concern. "Mr. Preston! Welcome. Amber told me you were coming with your wife." Her gaze moved to Sheila and her eyes bulged. "Do you know each other? This is Ryan Preston, our super talented renovator!"

Sheila grinned.

Ryan exclaimed, "This is my wife!"

Alicia's jaw dropped. She recovered and gasped, holding one hand to her chest, "I am *so* sorry! I had no idea!" Turning back toward the kitchen, she called "Amber! He's here!" Turning back to them, she added, grinning, "With his wife."

When Amber Branson came out, Alicia cried, "Did you *know* that Sheila is Ryan's wife?"

Amber's eyelids fluttered, and she shook her head. "I did not! Why didn't you tell us, Sheila?" She motioned them to a table.

Sheila blushed. She hadn't mentioned her husband because she hadn't known he was doing work for them. She didn't want to admit that. She merely smiled demurely. "Sorry."

"No matter. We know now." Amber leaned in. "Has he shown you the new addition? We absolutely love it!" She stopped to direct a beaming look upon Ryan. "I am thrilled beyond words. If it wasn't for your husband coming to me and suggesting the add-on, it wouldn't have happened. And it's precisely what I always wanted!"

While Sheila smiled proudly at her husband, Alicia said, "Does this mean I have to call you Mrs. Preston now?"

Ryan chuckled. "It means you can call me Ryan."

Alicia gave one of her wide smiles. "Oh! Thank you, Mr. Preston, er, Ryan."

Amber said, "Give Alicia your order and then come take a look. She'll let you know when it's ready." To Alicia she said, "It's on the house."

"Yes, ma'am," Alicia said with a smile.

"Thank you," Sheila and Ryan said. Amber waved her hand dismissively.

Alicia took their orders, and they went to join Amber who had moved off toward the new section. "Tales and Teacups," she told Sheila. "That's what we're calling it. It has its own entrance, so the sign will be over that." Still smiling she said, "I couldn't have asked for a better design or for a faster turnaround on one."

Ryan said, "Perfect. That's what I like to hear."

"Your husband is amazing. He knows how to get a job done."

"I know it," Sheila said, turning to beam at him. She was so proud!

"It's all about hiring the right help and giving the right leadership," he said. "It wasn't just me."

Amber waved her arm toward the interior. "I'm sure he's told you all about it, but here we'll have a full coffee bar. Over there," she pointed to another counter with display cases filled with delectable desserts, scones, and other goodies, "is our baked goods area. We're also preparing to offer soup and a selection of sandwiches."

"It looks wonderful," Sheila said.

They passed two displays of stationery gifts, bookmarks, and other bookish things and Sheila saw the rest of the largest room was a bookstore. Further in, Amber explained, was a room for private parties, and off to the side, a reading room with cubicles and device hookups.

"I want us to give Star Ones a run for the money!" she exclaimed, referring to the big chain of coffee shops that were all over the nation. "We're going to be the Aspen Creek go-to for coffee and conversation, books and reading."

The area was bursting with new, bright, shiny and yummy looking inventory. The architecture kept the old-world feeling with its newly polished mahogany trim, a copper-tiled ceiling inlaid with a lovely geometric design, and huge domed windows, letting in plenty of light.

Amber patted Sheila's arm and said, "I hope both our new businesses explode. Your husband's and ours."

"I do too," Sheila said, and she meant it with all her heart.

Ryan continued to walk her through, rubbing his hands together. "I was so excited to do this," he said, his eyes sparkling. "Even with the hired help, I got to do a lot of the finer work. I loved it, the feel of the tools, the finished woodwork, the hands-on stuff I stopped doing as a manager. I had a lot of talks with God," he continued. "But that was my problem. I did all the talking. I wasn't listening."

Sheila squeezed his arm.

"It gave me a sense of peace, though, to restore this place." He looked around, at the ceiling, nodding his head. "I felt like this is what I was really meant to do. Restoration. Beautification. Rebuilding." He looked at Sheila. "I think while I was rebuilding, it was rebuilding me. God was rebuilding me."

"I noticed you were coming home happier and with energy. I was glad that you were, but it bothered me not to know why."

He put his arm around her and drew her to his side. "I'm so sorry." He kissed the side of her head. "Never again." he said.

Alicia came hurrying toward them and motioned with her hand toward the café.

"Let's eat," Ryan said. "Then I'll show you my 'headquarters' outside of town."

She loved the sense of satisfaction and pride she heard in his voice.

While they ate, she asked, "What is Amber doing with the upstairs floors?"

His eyes sparked. "I'm working on a contract for that. She wants me to make them into two apartments which she'll rent out. Alicia has already expressed interest in the lower one. It would save her commute time, and she could easily work more hours."

"That sounds perfect for her!" Sheila exclaimed.

He nodded. "I'll need to get permits for a separate side entrance, first. We took out the staircase from the store area, and I'll need to put one outside. If we can't get the permits, we can't do it."

Chapter Twenty-Two

CHRISTMAS

THE NIGHT OF THE Christmas Eve service at Grace Church arrived. Sheila had her crockpot of savory meatballs in the church kitchen along with half a dozen others that members had brought and plugged in, ready to take to Gabe's after church for the annual potluck.

Like most of the congregation, she reveled in the one-hour service. The overhead lights were off, but softly glowing miniature bulbs from four green firs and the huge wooden cross at the back of the raised dais and podium gave the sanctuary an aura of reverence.

The worship leader led them in celebratory Christmas carols, and her heart went up to God in prayer even while singing. She and Ryan held hands during prayer from the pulpit, and even the kids were silent and touched by the atmosphere of holiness. God had sent His Son to earth for our sins to be forgiven. They seemed to understand even at their young ages, as everyone must, that it was for *their* sins personally.

When Sheila read from the children's Advent devotional each night, they ended in prayer. The children gave thanks for something that day and then confessed their sins for forgiveness. There was no better sleep remedy, she believed, than getting right with God before turning out the lights.

Surveying the congregation across the room, she felt bad for Emma. She had waved at her from the other side of the sanctuary, but her face was drawn. Sheila hoped to speak with her at the potluck. Ethan, recovering from his accident, was at home—Gabe's, that is, where he was staying. Emma was still battling with her heart and head over him and Gabe.

Really, Sheila thought, was it not to battle with the Lord as well?

Gabe didn't look any happier, and neither did Tessa.

We sure know how to make our lives messy, she thought. Emma was planning on accepting Gabe's ring—temporarily—even though she loved Ethan. And Tessa was planning on quitting the job she loved because she loved Gabe who was proposing to Emma. If that wasn't a mess, she didn't know what was.

She prayed, as she often had of late, that God's will would be done in their lives, and for clarity and wisdom to handle their dilemmas. She sent up a quick prayer for resolution this very night, Christmas Eve, when Emma would have to make her decision.

AT GABE'S HOUSE, THE children scurried around with the other youngsters and hardly ate a thing. Tessa, sitting beside her grandmother, looked troubled, her lips set in a grim line. Gabe and Emma looked equally miserable, and now even the usually jolly Ethan seemed on edge too.

Whether it was from pain from his injuries, or pain on Emma's account, she couldn't tell. Probably both. His leg was in a cast, one arm was bandaged, and another bandage was on the side of his face. She was thankful he hadn't been hurt worse.

Brielle and Leon came up to her holding hands and with big smiles. Brielle said, "Congratulations on your new company. 'Sheila Construction,' I love it!"

Sheila smiled. "Thank you, I was shocked he named it for me." Turning to Leon, she said, "Thanks for your help and support. And congratulations for being the silent partner!"

Leon smiled. "Thank you very much. Your husband's a good man with a good head on his shoulders." He smirked and added, "He's not half bad at construction, either."

They chuckled. Ryan came up behind her and put his arm around her. She turned to give him a loving look. He kissed her cheek and turned to the other couple.

"How's my business partner and his lovely bride-to-be?" As they continued chatting Sheila reflected that only three short days ago, she had hardly believed it would be a merry Christmas. Her and Ryan's love had been hidden by layers of distrust, secrecy, and hard circumstances, but it had been there, strong as ever, underneath it all.

Glancing at Emma, Tessa, Gabe and Ethan, she hoped and prayed there was a Christmas miracle in store for them too.

She couldn't stay to find out. Emma barely had time to whisper fiercely to her, "I know what I have to do!" before Jase came and hung on her dress, whimpering. He'd taken a fall and his arm, beneath his shirt, had a scrape. Sheila was wild to know if Emma's whisper meant she had come to her senses and wouldn't accept a proposal she did not want, but Kace joined the whining, complaining her friends were gone and she wished to go 'h-o-o-ome.'

Sheila wasn't eager to leave, but Jase was overtired and hurt. Kace was tired and getting grumpy. She and Ryan knew beforehand their evening would be cut short—that's the way it went with kids. And really, they didn't mind. They'd have time to sit before the fire together with hot drinks and contemplate the season and be lovey-dovey before putting out the gifts for tomorrow.

After many a hug and hearty, "Merry Christmas!" they went home around nine o'clock.

On Christmas Day, it wasn't unusual to talk with Emma at some point. They'd talk about the gifts they'd received and the ones they'd given. They'd find out what the other was cooking and whether they were eating at home or with relatives. This year Sheila planned on calling her friend earlier than usual. She was anxious to know what Emma had chosen to do about Gabe and his proposal, considering her feelings for Ethan.

Emma beat her to it, calling mid-morning.

"Merry Christmas and guess what! I'm engaged!" she cried, happily.

Sheila was less effusive. "Congratulations. I guess."

"No, I'm not engaged to Gabe! Ethan asked me to marry him!"

Sheila gasped. She could hardly believe it. "Oh. My. Gosh. I'm soooo happy for you."

Emma said, "I went outside expecting Gabe but it was Ethan! He kissed me and he proposed, and I said yes! I love him so much, Sheel."

"I know you do! I'm so relieved! Is Gabe okay?"

"He's more than okay. He knew it was coming; and it turns out he's sweet on Tessa! I'm glad for her sake. She's been soft on him for ages."

Sheila couldn't smile any wider. Both her friends' dilemmas were settled in one night! She'd prayed for that, but hadn't thought it could happen. *O she of little faith.*

"I want to tell you the whole story, but I don't want to keep you from your family on Christmas," Emma said. "And I'm getting ready to go see Ethan at Gabe's. But I had to let you know first."

"You sure did! Thank you. I've been anxious for you and Gabe, *and* Tessa and Ethan."

"I know. Thanks, Sheel."

"You just made my day! Come for dinner this week and bring Ethan. I can't wait to hear all about it."

"I can't wait to hear more about Sheila Construction. I saw Tales and Teacups; Ryan's work is gorgeous!"

Sheila couldn't wait to speak to Tessa to hear her story, too.

A FRESH SNOW STARTED falling midafternoon—perfect holiday weather. Ryan suggested they build a snowman in the front yard. To his surprise, the kids hesitated—they had new stuff they were enjoying. But soon the whole family bundled up and went outside for some front yard snowman building.

While the kids added stick arms and patted their finished creation with satisfaction, Ryan drew Sheila close. "Hey, did you notice the mistletoe overhead?"

Sheila looked up. There was cloudy sky and a few snowflakes trickling down.

She shook her head, smiling.

"You don't see it?" he asked, looking up as if it was right there in the air. He pointed straight up. "There, there it is."

"You don't need mistletoe to kiss me," Sheila said.

"It just makes it more fun," he said, leaning his head in and hovering his mouth near hers.

"But we have to make it short," Sheila said, taking a speedy look around. "We're in the front yard. The neighbors!"

"I couldn't care less about the neighbors," he said instantly. "I only care about you. About us." He bent his head again and kissed her softly but firmly on the mouth.

A few seconds ticked past and then Kacie's voice, full of glee. "Look, Jase, Daddy's doing it again! He's kissing Mommy like the prince in Cinderella!"

Chapter Twenty-Three

FRIENDS AND A FAREWELL

DINNER WAS IN THE oven for their big Christmas meal. The kids were relaxing while "The Christmas Story" played on TV. Sheila wore a new necklace with a diamond heart. After she had opened it and gasped, Ryan took it and put it around her neck. He closed the clasp and then nuzzled her neck with his lips. "Do you like it?"

"I love it! Thank you. But how did you afford it?"

"Well," he said in his deep soft voice, "I didn't put that *whole* five thousand into the business." Teasingly, he asked, "Does it make you feel blessed?"

"Y-e-e-es," she said slowly, as if she wasn't sure.

He turned her around to face him. "But?"

She held the necklace up so she could admire it again. With a wry grin, she said, "Diamonds *are* a girl's best friend, but—"

"Yes?"

She grinned. "I already told you. Next to Jesus Himself, *you're* the best Christmas blessing, the one I've wanted and needed all year."

"It's been a tough year," he said. "For us, and our friends."

"I'll say. Emma was agonizing almost from the day she met Ethan. Tessa was heartbroken about Gabe all year, and even Gabe must have had a hard time, since he was going to propose to Emma out of a sense of honor when he had feelings for Tessa."

The children were still enthralled with their new things, playing quietly on the rug.

Sheila's eyes fell to the Nativity on the mantel over the crackling fire.

God had bestowed Christmas miracles on all of them, first in sending His Son, and then, with Him, blessing them in incredible, wonderful ways.

Could there possibly be a better Christmas?

THE WEEK FOLLOWING THE big day was filled with visits and fun. The day of their dinner with Emma and Ethan, Ryan took the kids sledding while Sheila prepared the food. She couldn't wait to see Emma and Ethan together. They'd probably be smiling idiotically at each other, just like she and Ryan had done when they were engaged.

She fed the kids early and sent them downstairs to play while Ryan gave them strict instructions. They could come up to greet their guests but then had to play quietly downstairs or in their bedrooms until bedtime. Sheila put snacks and a drink for them in the playroom so they wouldn't come asking for them. The plan was for the adults to have a leisurely and undisturbed meal.

Over dinner, Emma and Ethan gladly shared their accounts of what happened on Christmas Eve. They all marveled at how well it had turned out, not only for them but for Gabe and Tessa as well.

Sheila enjoyed how comfortable the pair were with each other, and the rapt look on their faces whenever one watched the other as they spoke. Love was virtually oozing from both their gazes.

Emma held up her beautiful engagement ring and told the story she'd learned from Tessa. The poor besotted secretary had had to help Gabe pick it out for Emma, a painful thing for Tessa to do. But she'd chosen her second favorite ring, and Gabe had sold it to Ethan when he realized simultaneously, that he and Tessa were meant for each other, and Emma and Ethan were in love. He planned to get Tessa her favorite ring. The couple had probably already done that.

To Emma, the "second favorite" ring was perfect.

Then she and Ryan got to tell Emma and Ethan in detail how Sheila Construction came about. Ryan didn't skip his culpability about the secrecy, admitting that he'd allowed insecurities from his past to rule the day. He shared how the word of God had finally corrected him, and his only regret was that it took him so long to open up and listen.

Emma and Ethan had nothing but praise for Tales and Teacups, calling it "gorgeous work." They complimented Ryan for his vision, execution, and most of all, how quickly he'd got the job done. Emma chuckled with Sheila about how they'd heard the work going on, but neither had dreamed that Ryan was behind it.

"But you caught on first," Sheila reminded her. "While I was completely blind."

As Ryan spoke about the project, Sheila loved the energy and excitement that lit his handsome, chiseled face. His flirty shadow of a beard had already appeared, and she enjoyed just looking at him as he talked.

"Will you keep doing that kind of hands-on work?" Ethan asked.

Ryan rubbed his chin. "I'm wondering about that myself. I love doing it, getting absorbed in it, turning off the outside world while I work. I love the feel of the wood, the tools, and the satisfaction of a job well done."

"But I'm designing a model house right now, drawing up the plans. And I have four alternative plans in mind with customizations available. I'm hoping that once I get a few good contracts under our belt, I'll qualify for a real estate loan and put up a housing development. Only the model will be built ahead of time. The rest will go up as they're sold, customized for the owners. I'll use my hands-on skills at home, or for friends."

"A housing development, wow!" Emma said. "Will it be an HOA?"

Ryan shook his head firmly. "No HOA. Just a family-friendly development on one-acre lots with a walking trail. Plenty of room for kids, pools, whatever the homeowner wants." He paused and added, "I'm looking for an artist to draw up the model in full color for prospective buyers until it's built."

Emma looked at Ethan, her brows raised.

"That's not my area of expertise," he said. "It's yours!" He turned to Ryan. "You should see the houses she draws. Or paints."

Emma smiled. "Thank you, but I must *see* a house to draw it. I can't conjure one up, even if he described it to me."

"Let's try. I'll describe one to you and see how you do." Looking at the others, he said, "She is *really* good. I think she ought to sell her work."

"Let me know if you want to give it a stab," Ryan said. "For now, this is a back burner project anyway, because I have two new contracts to fulfill first."

The couple congratulated him. As Sheila brought out the mini stollens for dessert, the rest of the Christmas chocolates, and what Emma had brought—another plate of her mother's scrumptious chocolate star cookies—she sighed with contentment.

Her friends were happy. Her husband was happy and back to his old self—but even better. Their marriage was great. The kids were great.

Life was good.

God was good!

THE FOLLOWING SUNDAY—ETHAN'S LAST day as he was flying back to L.A.—the two engagements were announced from the pulpit by Pastor Mark. Gasps, astonished looks and a deep silence made Sheila nervous for the couples' sakes, so she stood and began clapping. Ryan immediately followed suit, as did Brielle and Leon.

In seconds, the congregation joined them, augmenting the applause with cheers, hoots and whistles.

"That's more like it," Pastor Mark said, grinning. "These are joyous tidings, and we are called to rejoice with them who rejoice."

She missed speaking to Tessa after the service, as she wanted to wish Ethan farewell, but she wasn't alone in that. He'd been there for almost four weeks and in that time had won more than Emma's heart. His cheerful generosity, uncomplaining attitude when he got injured, and all-around upbeat personality made him a favorite with many.

The goodbyes were earnest and full of well wishes. Gabe invited people to help him send Ethan off with prayer. Sheila joined Emma and the others who came up to pray over him for a full recovery from his injuries, traveling mercies and for his and Emma's coming marriage.

They were going to find it challenging to carry on a long-distance relationship until their wedding but were ready to do it. Ethan had suggested a quick marriage ceremony so Emma could go with him to L.A., where he lived. They'd have a big, second ceremony and reception in Aspen Creek later, but she refused.

She wasn't quite ready to leave Aspen Creek though the day was likely to come. In the meantime, Ethan would fly back and forth as time allowed. L.A. was a long trip from Aspen Creek, Pennsylvania.

They hadn't decided for certain where they'd live yet, and Sheila could only pray her best friend wasn't about to disappear to the other side of the country for good, but Ethan was a movie set designer and made a good living there. That was her only sorrow about the match. Not having her best friend nearby. They'd have to stay in touch by phone and facetime online.

Epilogue

Six months later

News of Ethan's beautiful renovation of the two stories above Tales and Teacups swept through Aspen Creek, bringing many jobs for Sheila Construction. The work wasn't for the new homes that Ryan hoped to build, but every job was significant and brought new referrals. Business was steady.

Sheila learned the software quickly and loved working for her namesake company. She was able to do most of the scheduling and calls right from the house—now sharing Ryan's office—and was always home when the kids got out of school, even on days when she went out to their rented "headquarters."

Alicia took the second floor apartment, and was known for disappearing at quiet moments from Maple & Main to show off her new home whenever anyone she knew came in and asked her to. Amber tolerated these small absences because she was just as pleased and proud of how the apartments turned out as her renter.

The third floor was occupied by a woman named Holly Berry, who had managed to convince Amber to give her a month-by-month rental agreement rather than an annual lease. Everybody instantly surmised that she must be the owner of the old Holly Berry Inn that had stood empty and decaying for two decades outside of town. Or maybe she'd inherited it, because she was only in her mid-twenties.

Then word got out that she was staying only long enough to have the old place demolished, after which she'd sell the land. Ryan wanted to nab that land as soon as it became available so he could build a model home on it for all to see. He'd already spoken to Ms. Berry about it. Sheila was planning to invite her for dinner so they could discuss it further.

Today, she'd only had one phone call to make before calling it a day. Her mother would arrive in time to watch the kids in case she was late, so she intended to browse through Tales and Teacups—she hardly ever seemed to have time for that—and then Ryan would join her for lunch at Maple & Main.

Alicia, her hair disheveled and cheeks high with color, greeted her warmly. Beside her was a strikingly pretty, petite, dark-haired woman, probably in her late twenties.

"This is Rosa, our new baker for Tales and Teacups," she explained. To Rosa she said, as though speaking to a child, "This is Shee-la."

"Shee-la, *hola*," she said shyly.

Sheila was struck by how attractive she was. Slim, small, and smooth-skinned, Rosa's dark hair was in a bun, but she could see it was shiny and thick. Her small nose and chiseled, delicate mouth, light tan, intelligent eyes and soft brows in a perfect arch, gave her the well-groomed look of someone who'd be comfortable in upper management of a company or weekend yachting. And here she was, a small-town baker for Tales and Teacups.

"She only speaks Spanish," Alicia explained, "but we're going to work with her to learn English. She's an out-of-this-world baker!" She pointed at the baked goods counter, where a smartly dressed man awaited his order while the cashier rang it up.

Alicia's brows rose in surprise, and she covered half her mouth in one hand. "Ooh, that's Mr. Caravelle," she whispered. "He was curious about the new store and came by yesterday to check it out. He bought a few goodies and raved about them!"

She grimaced. "Well, it was sort of a rave. He loved them. But I guess Mr. Caravelle doesn't rave about anything. He's very serious."

"Is he a local?" Sheila asked, surveying the slim man with dark hair in black pants and a business shirt. He held a briefcase in one hand.

"He owns the Mansion!" she exclaimed.

"Oh, wow," Sheila said. The Mansion was well known in Aspen Creek as it sat on a prominent hill and was an architectural diamond with its huge proportions, massive columns and covered portico in front. A line of low mountains was its backdrop, and it appeared in full view from a distance to travelers on the state highway. Aspen Creek was proud of its mansion. If Mr. Caravelle owned it, Sheila figured he must be super wealthy.

To Rosa, Alicia said slowly, "Sheila's hus-band de-signed this store." She waved expansively at the new rooms filled with pretty, appealing displays.

Rosa smiled politely, but Sheila guessed she hadn't understood a word. It was natural to feel that speaking slowly would help a person understand one's language, but that often wasn't the case.

She said, "Emma studied Spanish for years. Maybe she can help Rosa."

"Oh, that would be wonderful!" Alicia exclaimed. "Please ask her. Well, we've got to run. I have to get Rosa back in the kitchen."

At just that moment, Mr. Caravelle approached them. "This is the woman who bakes for you?"

He was younger than Sheila expected, probably no older than thirty, tall, ruddy and handsome. In a Clark Gable, business-suit sort of way. He surveyed Rosa, who looked questioningly at Alicia.

"Yes," she beamed, proudly. "We just hired her. Isn't she wonderful?"

"She certainly is." He pursed his lips. Looking at Rosa he said, "I need a baker at the Mansion. I'll pay you twice what you're getting here, and if you need room and board, we can work that in. I also give year-end bonuses and three weeks' vacation."

Alicia's jaw dropped. She put one hand on her hip and one protectively on Rosa's arm. "Mr. Caravelle," she said indignantly, "we've just hired Rosa and she works for *us*."

Probing eyes surveyed her. "Let's let her decide, shall we?" He turned to Rosa, whose face was tense. She bit her lip uncertainly. She'd caught the tone of Alicia's voice and didn't know what the issue was, but she knew it must concern her.

"She doesn't speak English," Alicia said curtly. "She didn't understand a word of what you just said."

He didn't blink or skip a beat. "I'll get an interpreter here tomorrow." He held the bag of goodies up for Rosa to see and smiled, pointing at them.

Rosa understood that and nodded her thanks, but her brows were knit. Even Sheila could feel the tension in the air.

Mr. Caravelle's sharp gaze lingered a second longer on the petite woman. "I'll see you tomorrow," he said to Alicia, who was glaring at him. To Rosa he said, "*Hasta mañana.*"

She smiled weakly at the unexpected Spanish and nodded uncertainly.

As Mr. Caravelle strode off—he walked with utter confidence, Sheila noted—Alicia huffed out a breath. "The nerve of that man! Imagine coming here to steal our new employee! Wait until I tell Amber."

"Is she here?" Sheila asked.

"No, she's home with a cold."

She smiled at Rosa, who gave her a shy but genuine smile in return before allowing Alicia to turn her toward the kitchen. Sheila wished she'd been a better student at Spanish. Rosa seemed nice.

Walking further into the new store, she felt that good things were happening in Aspen Creek. New renovations by their company for two businesses were scheduled to begin in a week, and down payments on the work had already come in. The businesses were right on Main Street, so Ryan's facelifts to the storefronts would be very visible—instant advertising for Sheila Construction.

As for Rosa, she hoped that Amber would fight to keep her new employee, but for Rosa's sake, was glad an interpreter would outline the better terms of Mr. Caravelle's offer. The woman could choose what was best for her.

She spent almost ninety minutes browsing and bought two books for herself and one each for the kids. Books were a worthy investment. Afterward, she texted Ryan to drive over so they could eat together. Over lunch, she told him what had happened with Rosa and Mr. Caravelle.

"Amber mentioned her to me," he said, swallowing a bite of a triple grilled cheese sandwich. "She worked for the government in Colombia, and was brought here by missionaries. They got her out just in time to save her from being forced into a drug cartel's compound. She's single and lives with another Spanish woman until she can get her mother here. She's hoping she can, anyway."

Sheila's eyes widened. "I wonder what she did in the government. And here she's a baker. I hope she's not unhappy."

He shook his head. "She had credentials, Amber wasn't sure what they were, but she couldn't transfer them here. But she loves to bake, so this is okay for now."

They continued eating. He said, "From what I've heard about Mr. Caravelle, he's a fair employer, but a businessman through and through. The mansion has been in his family for a hundred and fifty years. Somehow, he's always adding to his net worth.

"Is he married?"

Ryan's eyes lit with amusement. "Why do women always ask that question?"

She grinned. "Because Rosa's beautiful. If she works for him, I could see a romance in the future."

He tilted his head, thinking. "I doubt it. From what I've heard, Caravelle's got no time for romance. He's a workaholic."

"We'll see," said Sheila, as match-making wheels turned in her brain. "Aspen Creek is a romantic place. And there's a first time for everything."

She smiled impishly.

Ryan thought it was so cute that, if not for the table between them, he would have kissed her right there.

Coming in 2026!

AN ASPEN CREEK CHRISTMAS, BOOK 4

Rosa's trying to learn English and earn enough money to send for her mother from South America. A talented baker, when she accepts a job in Aspen Creek's mansion for a no-nonsense, grumpy businessman, she unwittingly turns his life—and heart—upside down!

Watch for Rosa's story, March 2026

Afterword

In Case You Wondered

It may have surprised you to to read about some of the groceries Sheila was able to find in the church food pantry. Let me explain.

Some food pantries, perhaps most, only supply canned or packaged shelf-stable items. Sheila's church received surplus food nearing it's "use by" or "best by" date from area restaurants and other food supply outlets that can no longer sell it.

Thus, fresh fruit, vegetables, milk, cream, frozen meat, pizza dough—anything could be on the menu on a given week.

My own church has a food pantry like this, only we don't call it a food pantry. As in the book, we call it simply "The Common Room."

Members also donate unwanted household items, books, stationery, and other things that are in very good to excellent condition, so other members who may need or want such items can take them at will.

It's a simple way for members to love on each other by donating good things.

If your church doesn't have such an "inside" ministry, consider starting one!

You could even go a step further and start a food pantry or common room open to the public.

About the Author

Linore Rose Burkard is an award-winning author who loves to craft clean love stories and happy endings that fill a sweet spot for readers who savor them.

Best known for Inspirational Regency romance, Linore's first book with Harvest House Publishers (*Before the Season Ends*) opened the genre for the CBA! Influenced by Georgette Heyer, Linore's historical romances are light-hearted fare steeped in Regency authenticity and faith.

A *magna cum laude* **English Lit grad from CUNY,** Linore now resides in southwestern Ohio with her husband and five (grown) kids, a cat and a Shorkie. She misses the beaches of Long Island but loves the wonderful hiking trails of her adopted state.

In addition to writing, Linore is a writing coach, Indie publisher, and President of the Dayton Christian Scribes. As her alter ego L.R. Burkard, she writes apocalyptic suspense. (*The Pulse Effex Series*)

For a free historical romance novel by Linore, join her mailing list at www.LinoreBurkard.com

I'd love to stay in touch, and you'll be among the first to know of sales, giveaways, freebies and writing updates! I'll never flood your inbox, and your email is safe with me, never shared or distributed in any way.